Born in Barcelona in 1931, **Juan Goytisolo** is Spain's greatest living writer. A bitter opponent of the Franco regime, his early novels were banned in Spain. In 1956, he moved to Paris and has since written novels, essays and two volumes of autobiography. *Landscapes after the Battle, Makbara, The Virtues of the Solitary Bird* and his extraordinary trilogy, *Marks of Identity, Count Julian* and *Juan the Landless* are also published by Serpent's Tail. Juan Goytisolo now lives in Marrakesh.

**Peter Bush** is the translator of Nuria Amat, Juan Carlos Onetti and Luis Sepulveda amongst others. He is also director of the British Centre for Literary Translation at the University of East Anglia in Norwich.

**Also by Juan Goytisolo and published
by Serpent's Tail**

*Landscapes After the Battle*
*Makbara*
*The Virtues of the Solitary Bird*
*Marks of Identity*
*Count Julian*
*Juan the Landless*

# The Garden of Secrets

As written down by
JUAN GOYTISOLO

Translated by Peter Bush

Funded by the Arts Council of England and
translated with the support of the European Commission's
Ariane 1999 programme.

Library of Congress Catalog Card Number: 00–100224

A catalogue record for this book is available from
the British Library on request

First Spanish edition Alfaguara 1997

First published in English in 2000 by Serpent's Tail,
4 Blackstock Mews, London N4 5BT

Website: www.serpentstail.com

Phototypeset in Bembo by Intype London Ltd
Printed in Great Britain by Mackays of Chatham, plc

10 9 8 7 6 5 4 3 2 1

'The most beautiful garden is a cupboard filled with books.'
*Tales of A Thousand and One Nights*

# FIRST WEEK

# ALIF

On the basis of a short review of a work whose author I'd
rather not remember, referring to the discovery in a suitcase
without owner of two quite distinctive series of poems
attributed without proof to Eusebio★★★, interned at the
request of his family in the military psychiatric centre in
Melilla at the start of the July '36 rebellion, from which
he escaped, according to one version, aided and abetted by
a soldier from the Rif, or where, according to another, he
underwent 'rehabilitation treatment' provided by a few
Fascist psychiatrists, we, a Circle of active, passionate readers
in a provincial city, decided to write a collective story based
on the poet's elusive history, gathered together over the
course of three weeks in the benign summer shade of a
delightfully cultivated garden.

The backgrounds, professions, interests and political ideas
of the readers' group were as various as the clouds in the
sky. They included journalists, cinema buffs, fledgling
writers, students from Spanish and North American
creative writing schools, sociologists, lawyers, ethnologists,
a graduate in Arabic language and literature, a specialist in
the language of Quevedo, two assiduous readers of Ibn Arabi
and other mystical, esoteric writers. One of them, a
devotee of the Houroufi sect influenced by the Kabbala and
Pythagoras's theories, presented its numerical interpretation

of the Arabic alphabet and its relationship with the human face to impose double the fourteen letters it comprises, that is, twenty-eight – a number equal to the characters of the Arabic alphabet – on the number of storytellers in the Circle: we should be twenty-eight, no more or less, our scribe-cum-secretary and bibliographer included. Some of us had followed the twists and turns of the far left from hard-line Marxism-Leninism to harmless, utopian anarchism, the majority declared itself apolitical and one man supported the ideals and rallying calls of the far right. Had they but known, feminists of the stripe of Kate Millett and Ms Lewin-Strauss would have justifiably condemned the group's composition: it contained only four women.

Their literary tastes were equally different and embraced a wide range of schools: from traditional or behaviourist realism to tales of dreams and fantasy. Some preferred a personal narrative, others opted for the third person singular. Eusebio's character was usually seen from the outside, sometimes from within, and occasionally, from the sidelines or *en passant*. The collaborative project was based on the systematic demolition of that disposable entity, the novelist, a happy, liberating dispensation.

The co-readers' aim was to put an end to the oppressive, pervasive notion of the Author: each of us had complete freedom to tell our story, to follow the thread of our predecessor's exposition or to unauthorise it and switch the drift. The Circle's ambition was to realise a creative mix of perspectives and possibilities, in movement from one chapter to another across shifting, uncertain frontiers. In the parleys prior to the assembly of the novel we registered the existence of two opposing tendencies: one trying to pursue a straight or zig-zagging story-line, constructing the character in fits and starts: another favouring a densely foliaged narrative, with digressions and alternatives which, from a fertile central trunk, generated stand-alone or grafted-on stories.

Supporters of the first defended the hypothesis of Eusebio's 'rehabilitation' by the Movement's eugenicist psychiatrists for whom Marxism was a product of psycho-sexual degeneration; defenders of the second ventured on the sands of his apparent escape and the confused traces of his later life.

Our Cervantine garden, with its flower beds and borders, belonged also to Borges: forking paths, advancing, extrapolating, halting, turning back. This provoked tensions and even conflict among the readers, but the literary addiction uniting us in the end overcame any other consideration. After fierce debate we drew lots to decide the order of contributions from participants, alternated hypotheses and set the public storytelling on Fridays over three weeks: nine or ten tales per soirée.

That's how our Circle created these weeks in the garden out of absolute respect for each storyteller's inventiveness. Although the narrators' different points of view and variegated literary education led to a powerful centrifugal tendency, the thematic convention of clinging to Eusebio's character acted as check and counterbalance. As the Circle's secretary and anonymous scribe – I'll not reveal my name so that, in the words of one classic, 'detractors can best satisfy the gossip-mongers by not knowing whom to pillory' – my role was reduced to the structuring of what some avant-garde critic would call the 'hypertext', in accord with the roll-call of readings for our summery gatherings in the garden.

# BAA

The image tormented him, he couldn't shake it off: a prison
where those stricken by the red plague, packed in a shed
without natural light, enacted the twilight ritual of the
chains. While some remained night and day fixed to
the wall by links connected to their convicts' collars, most
put them on and shut them round their necks, awaiting
their turn to be connected to the links of the thick collective
chain: each slotted his collar on to the chain and passed
the links to his neighbour till they were one. But the human
cluster sometimes swayed frantically and the guards then
secured the calm of the disolocated centipede via extra
handcuffs and fetters. The army chaplain and an officer
supervised the orderly carrying-out of the operation: the
collective chanting of the Our Father, switching-off of
anaemic bulbs, brusque slamming of the main door.

Had he really lived that scene? Or was it simply a
nightmare, a side-effect of the doubtful sleeping pills they
gave him? After dreaming and convulsing, he languished in
absent self-absorption, totally alien to life, enwrapped by
the silent shadows. In flashes he evoked uncertain, dazzling
visions: robust invocations, howls of complaint, vain pleas
to the staff. He didn't know who he was, what he was
doing, where he was. Did he slaver from the corner of his
mouth like his room-mate? Had his attacks been that violent

to warrant the handcuffs and manacles he stared at obliquely, even horizontally? Hour after hour of anxiety-rent stupor, retreat to the protective maternal cloister, yet fear of brutal ejection. Had he again urinated unawares and would he again suffer the nurse's insults and reprimands? When would he burst into his pitch-black cell – for cell was what it was – and submit him to the rough therapy prescribed by his bosses? Was there any likelihood he might gain access to his medical records and see how his illness was progressing? Were his ideological-sexual deviations curable, as the establishment's lord and master had so definitively affirmed?

The blasts on the barracks bugle mingled with muffled resonances, intensifying his disquiet: patriotic marches, drum-banging, the hymn of the Foreign Legion. What had happened outside since he'd been interned? Why couldn't he communicate with his sister or get news from her? Had the uprising spread to the mainland or was it restricted to the military garrisons in Africa? Radio proclamations occasionally filtering in from the passage pointed to the existence of bloody warfare, lyrically described by its promoters as a Crusade. If the insurgents got their way, what would be the lot of Federico, Manolo and Concha, Luis, Emilio, of all his friends? Would they receive his kind of preferential treatment or would they be summarily executed like most people?

In lucid moments question after question pounded his brain, as the influence of sedatives wore off. But he soon relapsed into drowsiness, pits of unbearable pain, listening to the cries uttered by someone who was perhaps himself: hallucinations of dungeons, a string of prisoners, salvoes from endless executions, corpses piled into common graves, the hoarse shrieks of animals decapitated in the slaughterhouse.

Faces set in hatred, bellowing against the red plague, gun-happy soldiers, missals, mantillas, raised arms, Falangist berets, bullying little rich boys, pistols tucked under their belts, walked in and out of his nightmares, fleetingly crammed into his tiny cell, roamed the half dark like phantoms, nailed him to his sick bed.

For weeks or for months on end?

One day they untied the straps binding him to his bed, drew the curtains, let him get up and look through the window. The sickbay occupied one of the wings on the second floor of the massive barracks: a few recruits hurried to and fro, bantered, stood to attention when stripes and tassels passed by, gave messages to the guards, chatted next to the Chief of Staff's office or by the hectic main gate. The leaves of a solitary plane tree were turning yellow: summer was long gone.

From his narrow opening on to the world outside, he kept a sharp eye on everything that went by: the space was reduced to a rectangular yard of regulated monotony. In one period of rapt contemplation, his eyes lighted on one of the duty soldiers and intense emotion swept over him: his friend from Tabor, the one with the wild moustache, standing to attention, the butt of his sub-machine gun resting on the ground. The memory of their rendezvous in the studio lent by Federico's lover fired his heart: previous reality had not been obliterated; he could still cling to it tightly like a safety buoy. The youth's closeness brought back a past recent yet remote, nightly encounters in the painter's private lair: side by side, stretched out, pipes of kef on the sofa, ready to enjoy their coupling with its canny blend of strength, force and gentleness.

As soon as he could, he put his nose to the window and spied on the duty hours of his brother-in-law's former orderly, the main reason for his rash visit to Melilla on the

eve of the predictable, feared uprising. In spite of himself,
he cried and cried. How could he signal his presence to
him without drawing the nurses' attention or being subject
to new punishment and reprisals? Had his discreet pleas for
help brought his imprisonment to his notice, or, informed
by other means, was the *askari* waiting for the right
opportunity to help? The fact is that, taking advantage of the
bustle or oversight of the other soldiers or after a change of
guards, he blew him a kiss, insistently stroked his holy
of holies, a promising hint.

How long did that silent play between him and the *askari*
go on? Time sped by imperceptibly, unbearably. Impotence
sentenced him to deception: he tolerated without protest
painful injections and bitter draughts, pretended to be calm
and collected, showed deep respect towards the chaplain and
medical personnel. His friend had pointed the end of a
rope in his direction and he understood he was being invited
to cut loose. From then on, he spent all the time he could
easing out, but not breaking, the glass from one side of the
window, the catch of which had been rendered useless by
a pre-emptive nail. He counted the days and nights waiting
to be alerted to his freedom. He – the timid, tremulous,
shrinking violet – felt full of energy and courage. When he
finally spotted the agreed signal, he carefully removed the
glass, grabbed the end of the rope thrown dead on target
from the yard, tied it to the lip of the catch and slid down
to the ground.

It was three a.m. and the other guard was snoring
drunkenly after downing the bottle of anis, a present from
his comrade. Then, everything happened quickly, followed
well-laid plans: his disguise as a woman from the Rif; the
showing of the military identity card at road blocks; the flight
across the countryside, along paths and short cuts familiar
to his saviour, on and into the French Protectorate.

# TAA

Me or the other?

You could see him from the outside, feet shackled,
strapped to his bunk to prevent any possible suicide attempt
or flight from the hospital torture rack, shuddering violently,
purged by the currents of therapeutic electricity.

How long had he stayed unconscious, recovering from
the electric shocks prescribed by the doctor after a careful
read of his clinical diagnosis?: 'a schizoid personality,
influenced by both physical and psychic pathogenic agents,
a victim of collectivist social utopias and delirium, feminoid
urges channelled by harmful reading and company towards
open sexual inversion'.

Had he shouted out in pain, howled like a wounded
animal, like the patient in the next rooms, as the currents
began to course through his inert body?

Through the slit between half-closed eyelids, you
glimpsed the walls of the odious cell, decorated only by a
crucifix and print of the Virgin Mary, minimal furniture of
side-table, chair, bed with your temperature chart and a
basin for your vomit and retchings which an expressionless,
taciturn female nurse had the job of emptying.

Sunk in profound lethargy, you tried in vain to remember,
to distinguish night from day, roughly gauge the time, predict
with silent apprehension the doctor's visit, the educational

chit-chat with the chaplain, and the preparations for a fresh, brutal session of treatment.

Had you been the victim of those who preach envy and hatred, who wish to undermine the foundations of family and nation, encourage bestial erotic groping, foment depravation and confusion of sexes, pawns in the grip of the Moscow International, red propagators of perversion and libertinage pursuing a coldly premeditated strategy to precipitate moral dissipation?

All inspired by a do-gooding liberal-Communist conspiracy against the values and creeds handed down by our blue-blooded ancestors. Marxist siren-songs trying to spread foreign ideas among us, scatter poisonous weeds over the field of our faith, give a rosy glow to cities swamped by foreigners, clear the ground for the foul tyranny of the envious hordes. Limp-wristed wimps like you are easily duped by the hypocrisy and guile of self-seekers, Jewish freemasons and pinko eunuchs: trapped, dragged into the whirlpool of the worst depravity. You're a poet, so they tell me: you could have praised God's breath of fire, the prophetic burning bush, the fatherland's noble soil, chaste, dignified women, fertile furrows and ears of corn, the sublime beauty of the eternal. But you were led into sin by that crew of traitors and pen-pushing mercenaries who, on the run, seek refuge abroad, cuddle up to the bosoms of their petty paymasters, or parade their radiophonic bluster on the wavelengths of the red peril. Their poetry is the muse in reverse, the perverts' perineal muse, coarse sand-swept desert songs, demagogic hot air without the pulse of poetry, oozing, plebeian pores, unnatural thrills, forbidden pleasures . . . Listen to me, Eusebio, suffering redeems and purifies. Your soul is in pain no more: only your body, your lacerated flesh. Pray, pray, beseech unto the Lord: break me even more, do what you will of me. Make my pain infinite

and let me feel the weight of your anger on my brow! If
I share an atom of your sufferings, increase them and silence
my moans!

You could see him by the bedhead of your double, day
after day after day, before and after the electric shocks,
grimly insistent, his face had faded from your memory, but
not the elongated, bony hands, the ugly, dirty nails, the
cunning wiles.

How long did the initial phase of your treatment last?

You were helped by no calendar, you'd lost the notion of
time, the cycles of anguish exhaustion torpor were
repeated, your family lost on a distant horizon, you had no
past, didn't know who you were. Once you heard the ditty
'Rocío, ay mi Rocío', perhaps sung in the passage by a
cleaning woman, and suddenly what was buried rushed to
the surface of memory, you started to cry uncontrollably,
again you heard the voice from the gramophone mixed up
with your sister's, both of you in the lounge of the spacious
villa in the military district on the eve of the events,
everything snatched from you in the dark course of a story-
line you hadn't written, but those tears did belong to you,
nobody but nobody could snatch them from you!

Come on, doctor!, he won't stop sobbing and shouting,
writhing in his strait-jacket, trying to throw off the straps,
administer a sedative.

Then you re-entered the void, were silent again, docile,
now they weren't giving you electric shocks, you remained
indifferent, in a kind of limbo, alien to all around, your eyes
staring at your shackled ankles.

Unreal, through the haze, you discerned the army
chaplain's face, his beret and medallion, the silver crucifix
pinned to his chest, rejoice, Eusebio, put the suffering
behind you, take up the staff of life, arise, move your lips,
praise God's mercy! your affliction reached the feet of the

Lord and he was moved!, one day, very soon, you'll be completely cured, you'll gladly be someone else and the poems pressed tight in your heart fighting to express themselves will extol God's glory and the greatness of our land, the firm helm of our Leader, the sacrifices of those fallen, the final victory of our righteous sword!

You don't know how long your senses were eclipsed. When you woke up, you were in another room, in the Medical Rehabilitation Centre, next to Comrade Basilio.

# THAA

My preliminary investigations into the whereabouts of
Eusebio★★★ and the *askari* accompanying him on his escape
led nowhere. As a result of the vicissitudes of the military
uprising that was supported by most diplomats and civil
servants in the Spanish Consulate in Casablanca, of which
the Marrakesh Medina was a dependency, the archives
disappeared or were destroyed. Those later restored, in the
wake of the American landing and return of the Royal
Protectorate to the Gaullist embrace, are unfortunately
incomplete and contain only data of citizens who presented
themselves for registration there or made some contact with
it. In not one of the files preserved from the 1943–1955
period did I find a mention of his name, from which I
deduce he lived those years as a refugee or stateless.
Subsequent questioning of the minuscule colony of his
compatriots resident in the city over the last fifty years shed
no light either. None of his names or personal details meant
anything to them, rang the slightest bell.

As I was despairing of clarifying the mystery shrouding
the final stage of his life, a conversation with my good
friend the chemist Abu Ayub put me on the right track. An
octogenarian Frenchman who sometimes visits him –
formerly a teacher in his country's Cultural Centre and
translator of Tamazight poetry – once referred to his

memories of a Spaniard who cohabited for some twenty
years with a Beni Snasen in a humble dwelling in the
Kennaria district. His profile matched that of the poet you
sought, and, after numerous telephone calls and frustrated
appointments, I managed to interview the old man in his
garden house in Gueliz, its iron railings and pink façade
covered, almost suffocated by bulimic bougainvillea.

'If my memory serves me,' said Monsieur M.L., 'around
that date a Spaniard by the name of Eusebio settled in a
sidestreet in Riad Zitun Al Khadid, next to the street where
my late wife and I lived. He was a man in his forties, small,
fragile, poorly dressed and well-mannered, despite a natural
reserve and solitary ways. He shared two or three rooms
in a modest home with a wood-cutter and charcoal burner,
an ex-Foreign Legionnaire, whose sturdy, muscular frame,
tanned face and violent features, created an impression of
harshness exacerbated by his jet-black, bushy moustache:
an uncouth country fellow, an evil-looking, sly individual
feared by everyone.

'Although at first we took him to be his domestic, we
soon understood he wasn't: rather than his lover, Eusebio
appeared to be his servant. Abstemious and respectful of
Mohammedan law, he would buy demijohns of wine for
his friend in the bodega run by the Algerian near the Riad
Zitun arch, by the Saint's hermitage. He also saw to the
domestic chores and shopping in the market, where he
exchanged greetings with the natives, mingled his halting
French with recently acquired dialect. His friend went to
and fro with his cart laden with wood which he fed into
the charcoal stove, the product of which he sold by the
bushel after weighing it on an old steelyard.

'Their peculiar relationship at first attracted the attention
of the locals, but, unlike in Europe, people here talk about
everything but are shocked by nothing. The neighbours had

grown used to the *askari*'s shouts and insults to which
Eusebio never responded. The sound of voices, blows, whip-
lashes, groans sometimes went on till midnight and,
although the poet didn't hide his bruises and more than
once suffered from broken ribs, he never complained or
made reference to his continuous mistreatment.

'Rumours were rife that he had converted to Islam and
slipped into the Mosque to pray, silent and apart from the
others. His unkempt clothes and the djellaba he wrapped
round himself to ward off the cold confused visitors. After a
few years in the Medina, no stranger or newcomer took
him for a Gentile.

'The day he died, some colleagues and I went to the
wake, and the *askari*, usually so fierce and hot-tempered,
cried disconsolately, vehemently proclaimed his saintliness:
all his public activity – buying wine and even pretending
to drink it – obeyed his desire to castigate his pride and
maintain the ideal of secret perfection. He was the one
ordering his own punishment, suffering in silence, who
rapturously greeted the drubbing, happily kissed the hand
that oppressed him. More recently he rarely ate and
prolonged his fasting to the point of exhaustion. He
followed the precepts of Sidi Ben Sliman Al Yazuli to the
letter as to the indexes of prophetic graces. He would only
wear torn clothes and gave out his scarce coins to the aged
and to women more in need than himself. Renunciation
of material goods was his goal; poverty, his only honour.

'He was buried following Muslim rites on a hill near
Oued Nfis and, according to one young Tamazight, for
some time women from nearby Bedouin encampments have
visited his grave, anxious to obtain his blessing: a white
sepulchre, no inscription, adorned with the faithfuls' ex-
votos and knotted ribbons. His companion's, who died
grief-stricken shortly after, is alongside.'

That is all I could find out about him and his 'station' of renunciation and concealment.

Monsieur M.L. – whose narrative I've faithfully recorded and translated – isn't entirely sure if he continued writing poetry or if the verse now attributed to him is in fact his work.

'Here,' he pointed out, 'saints often leave disciples who adopt their name and link into their initiatory chain. Sufi poetry, like the ballads of your country, is by and large the fruit of a collective elaboration. The qasidas by Sidi Abderrahman Al Mahkdoub today belong to the whole people which recites them.'

I regret not gathering up more details about Eusebio★★★ or being able to check those proferred by my informant against anything more precise.

In T. where I went to visit his sepulchre, its inhabitants knew little about him: he was, they said, a Gentile who converted to their creed and followed the ascetic life of the Haddaoua and other brotherhoods expressing popular religiosity. His origins are also the object of controversy: some say he came from Garnata or Granada, others that he was probably French. They only agree on one thing: thanks to his charismatic intervention, barren women obtain, as in Mulay Brahim, the gift of fertility.

But as I draw to a close, I realise my findings don't shed light on the riddle perplexing us. I leave to my colleagues in the Readers' Circle the task of unravelling through their own explorations the destiny of a poet engulfed by the whirlpool of our merciless civil war.

# JEEM

HE DREAMT
  he was at the Beni Enzar frontier post in the hands of
insurgents, trying to bribe a lance-corporal, his brother-in-
law's ex-orderly, so he could go over to the other side and
avoid the stations of the cross to summary execution, to
the ritual *paseo*
  he fled a feverish city of clamorous loudspeakers and
unfurling flags, of lorries crammed with soldiers and
civilians raising their arms, of scenes of the persecution
and capture of government supporters guilty of Republican
sympathies, of avenging slogans and leaflets inciting patriotic
vigilance and denunciations
  the news of the coup being hatched had caught him far
from the protective ambit of his sister and brother-in-law,
in the studio of a painter-friend where he went to write his
poems and literary reviews or sleep with some soldiers
from Tabor
  patrols, hostages, control posts cut off the path to his only
point of refuge, from their cars little rich kids of the Falange
cheered their criminal generals in the midst of the rabble,
accumulated hatred and scorn surfacing on their vociferous
faces which scented prey and wanted blood
  long live Franco, Mola, Sanjurjo, the Legion and the
Army, death to Azaña and the red hordes, God is on our

side, we shall crush them, we shall cleanse Spain of the virus of socialism, we shall restore her imperial grandeur and Catholic unity

and suddenly

the rasping voice of a loudmouthed, leery officer, halt!, who let that element slip through, can't you see he's one of those sour pussies? collaborator to boot with the Marxist, atheist press, a red, a queer and a poet, can you imagine?, over here my little fruit-cake, stop your swanking, my fists'll give you a facelift, you don't deserve to be executed, the firing squad's for men and you hardly qualify, you wide-arsed mothersucker!

pushing, gobs of spit, insults as he invoked his brother-in-law, repeated his name and rank, lieutenant colonel in the Sappers, three times wounded in the Rif, Franco's companion-in-arms!

(had he moved while sleeping?, the nightmare went on now in a different milieu)

the military chaplain from the barracks hospital didn't look severely compassionate as usual, according to Basilio's criteria, but icy, implacable, angular, hard-edged, clad in monkish or inquisitorial habits slashed at the knee, damning his vices and deviations, the Vice, particularly odious to God and his angels, responsible moreover, as in other eras for the fatal decadence of the nation, the ruination of Spain

he read solemnly, like a prosecutor summing up, the Third Canon of the Sixteenth Council of Toledo held in the year 693 on the eve of the Saracen invasion:

'As in the past this horrendous, abominable crime led sodomites to be consumed by fire raining down from heaven, today it will also lead those guilty of committing the act, men going with men, against nature, to the flames of eternal damnation.'

he should repeat it, memorise it, give thanks to God for the providential intervention that had saved his life and kept him from hell, docilely submit to the tests which would dislodge the vice from his body, electric shocks associated with suggestive images, manacled, strapped to the bed, harsh therapy necessary for his cure and for oblivion, the will to be reborn, to be someone else, a soul regenerated by the ordeal of suffering, a peak of patriotic virtue, worthy of those martyred for God and for Spain, of their noble, selfless example

he slavered as his bulging eyes examined the bare walls of the room where he remained chained after the waves of electricity, trapped in his cell like a Jew in the snares of the Inquisition

shouted, almost howled, Basilio's talismanic name

woke up in a cold sweat to discover that his flat next to Sierpes had been transformed into a cage from which there was no escape

# HAA

When my dear friend, Madame S., learned of the reasons
for my visit to Marrakesh and the object of my enquiries,
she evoked a lonely man whose halting accent clearly
revealed peninsular, perhaps Levantine origins. For years
he'd lived in a small house in the Casbah, accompanied by
a native who entirely matched the one described in the
narrative. The likely Eusebio was a man of few words who
kept himself to himself: he had no contacts with the
European enclave and, despite Madame S.'s repeated
invitations, drawn by his reputation as a sage and ascetic,
she never managed to drag him along to her restaurant. The
only time she dared approach his house in Derb Chtuka,
bearing a letter with a confused address that, according to
the postman, had ended up at her establishment after
doing the rounds of the whole city, the recluse delayed
several minutes before answering her insistent bell-ringing
– 'he's in, he's in', had confided a neighbour, 'he always
takes his time', and, after undoing the bolt, there he was,
gone native, not inviting her to cross the sacred boundary
of his doorstep, menacingly silent. Visibly repelled, he bent
down to take the missive and said, guess what he said, she
immediately made a note so she wouldn't forget and later
copied it into her diary, yes these were his exact words,
'Seek out my traces, and you will find but your own

footprints', I'm telling it just as it was, before he bent down again, tore the letter into a thousand pieces and shut the door in her nose, a cruelly refined, gentle gesture. Just like that, *ma pauvre amie*, not adding a fullstop or comma, leaving me in the lurch in the street while a gang of kids pounced on the shreds of the remote, much-travelled message, fought ferociously over the remains. This was the Eusebio who so fascinated me, the man in hiding who kept his distance, furtive and prickly in his little house in the Casbah, zealous guardian of his precious privacy.

He had become a Muslim, sighed Madame S., the neighbours said he went to the Mosque on the brow of dawn and thanks to their confidences, cash loosens tongues, I discovered that he stayed there after canonical prayers, as if immersed, a greengrocer told me, the husband of one of my employees, in an ocean of perplexity.

The native servant, as taciturn and impregnable as his master, followed him like a shadow inside and outside the house, seemed to skim the ground, his moccasins never touching down. He was often to be seen laden with books and old manuscripts that Eusebio read and re-read till sleep overcame him and the candle spluttered out. Which books?, I asked my confidant from Derb Chtuka. Works by sages, poets and saints, submerged himself in them, daily absorption in the ambit of their veiled enigmas. He glides, levitates, returns to earth, listens to the music of the spheres, isn't afraid to lose, doesn't expect to win.

I carefully transcribed everything he said, encouraged him along a prying path and once saw him approach smiling slyly, with a fish he'd caught in his net, the corner of a handwritten card he clutched like a miraculous relic, Madame S., words in his very own hand, rewarding your long wait, about his stubborn search, whose signs he couldn't decipher, written in fine Gentile script, all for the modest price of a few riyals.

It was a poem in English, perhaps a translation, which I immediately passed on to one of my customers, a learned Londoner, with a degree in Hispanic literature, who read repeatedly, *then my bones, decayed, love you in the dust*, and then in Spanish, *polvo serán mas polvo enamorado*, a quote from memory, he pointed out, a profound, very beautiful poem by Quevedo, but, who on earth had imitated who?, and with the sample written in his book of relics he rushed over to see a bookseller sage in Bab Ksur, a great source of stories, legends and poems, and, on his return, his face glowed in a sibylline, philological halo, like an expert in the arts of falconry with his peregrine and its prey. He had identified the author but not solved the riddle, no reasonable explanation of the transmission, only aleatory amorous, mystic convergence, how could a poet from the time of Quevedo be inspired by Shibli's recondite work?

That was how I was able to peek at his reading-matter, dip into the opaque reaches of his life before the faithful, surly native servant died and the elusive object of my searches buried him in a district of Tahanaut where in his turn he went shortly afterwards, to be close to his sepulchre, in the same village where you went to visit him, please pour yourself another cup of tea, would you like some cakes?, I've got some delicious croissants exquisitely prepared by my cook.

Madame S. scrutinised me, beset with worry, hanging on the oracle of my words, not noticing that when I let rip I invented and lied to her, reluctant to share my experience before I'd committed it to writing, every dog to his bone, her nervous state in the end exhausted me.

How could I describe to her the effect of my immediate closeness to that clean, tidy old man with his handsome, almost manicured beard, framed by the dismal confines of his down-at-heel oil mill, totally oblivious to the world around him, cloistered between four stone walls, with his squalid, basic needs and rustic charcoal stove. Was our reality a mere metaphor in an insignificant corner of eternal existence? That is all I could think as he locked himself into his silence, sat on the earthen floor, stared at a point behind my back, as if he was unaware of my presence or my total lack of substance allowed him to see through me.

You are you and I am I, he said.

(I looked at his djellaba's delicate, slender hood, a perfect symmetry with the point of his beard.)

You are I and I am you.

(He stared at me, his irises like pearls set in glass.)

You are not I and I am not you.

I looked at him transfixed, drawn by the brilliance of his eyes.)

I am not you and you are not I.

(I felt myself crumbling under his gaze, being reduced to old copper coin.)

You are not you and you are no other but you.

(His gaze sentenced me to extinction, with no possible return to ephemeral contingency.)

We stayed hours days weeks silent and still.

The spiders swung from the corners of the press, ants ran over the greasy walls, kids broke the calm outside with the strident levity of their cries. Only the buzzing of the bees maintained the nodular boundaries of the circle encapsulating us, ensured its hesitant continuity.

The old man sat up, abruptly ended the interview.

He who has seen me has not seen me, he said.

I detatched myself from the brightness in his eyes and abandoned the dream. I'd read all that in Ibn Arabi. But how could I let on to dear old Madame S.?

# KHAA

'You are, my friend, Eugenio Asensio, you're born again, you've changed names and, for the good of Spain, your previous and devious personality.' Comrade Basilio smiled at him with the aplomb and rigour bestowed by rank. He wore the uniform of the Falange: red beret, boots, blue shirt, yoke and arrows. He had summoned him to his office and, for the first time since the events, somebody was addressing him, if not affectionately, at least warmly.

'By a whisker your brother-in-law's intervention saved you from meeting your Maker: you were on the list of Reds to be executed. Your poor sister wept her heart out, begged and begged till her husband gave in. That was when they took you from the garage where you were shoved cheek by jowl with those destined for the *paseo*, handcuffed and blindfolded, to get round the duty officer who wasn't in on the act. You can't imagine the stratagems your family's friends had recourse to, what obstacles they confronted to sneak you out of Melilla and bring you here in one piece. They saved you from the fate of Federico, a good lad when all's said and done, like you tricked by envy-ridden intellectuals and politicos in the pay of the Anti-Spain. Now you're in a safe haven and we'll do what was agreed. Put behind you who you were, your shameful penchant for Mohammeds and labourers, bad friends and twisted ideas.

From now on my comrades and I will see to it you become a wholesome man, wear the uniform expressing our all-embracing, combative spirit, strengthen yourself body and soul, espouse the values consubstantial with the fatherland forged by its martyrs' bloody sacrifice. Look at your new documentation: the dates haven't changed, your place of origin has. You were born in the Canary Islands, like our Army of Salvation. Your name is Eugenio Asensio García. Eugenio, because, as one of the luminaries of our thought writes, with characteristic rigour and lucidity, the eugenic cleansing and regeneration of a people has to impact on the totality of its constituent individuals, to create an ethnically improved, morally robust and spiritually vigorous caste. A eugenics to liberate individuals from damaging cancers and return them, via a programme of proper mental and physical hygiene, to the incubator, to germinate and blossom as in a greenhouse, forged against the corrupting environment, by the sacred store of principles firing our Crusade.

'I know what it means for you to cut all ties with a person of your sister's stature and capacity for love. She's in tears as well but feels happy and grateful to her husband. She has sworn to him she'll not try to contact you and I'll be responsible for informing her of your progression to a total cure. From now you'll be among men, the leaders and fighters of the Falange, determined to shape their lives after the example of their Founder. There's no room here for the moral scruples of English laydeez or any soft-soaping: this is no convent. The mannered ways of hypocrites and do-gooders are not our scene. Our life is one of obedience, discipline, militia: the militarisation of school, university, factory, workshop, of every pore of society. We don't want rewards, Laureates or Medals of Suffering for the Fatherland. Hierarchy is based on merit, selflessness and vigour in the service of Spain. By my side, by the side of

Veremundo and his doughty fighters, you'll learn the virtues of manliness, the longing after perfection of Greek philosophers and German artists. When it's time to work and do your duty, work and do your duty like the next man; when it's time to have a good time, on the razzle and the beer, enjoy yourself, satisfy the body. We won't force you to go to brothels if you're still in two minds and their ways put you off. But gradually we'll inculcate in you noble tastes and desires. Proper male camaraderie excludes all forms of hypocrisy and cant.

'Stop reading palsied prose, absorb the tough truths of José Antonio, the essays of Ramiro de Maeztú, Onésimo Redondo and Ledesma Ramos. Choose between the peaks and the abyss, between anarchy and the Renaissance ideal of the poet-soldier. Your bohemian, egg-head mentors generate castrated, masturbatory art: abstract drawings, dramas of adultery, trite, effeminate poetry, novels inciting class struggle. Tasteless, stinking fruit falling apart in the hands like rotten apples. Whoever sidesteps truth and denies the sap of our spirit misses out on beauty, inverts the proper scale of values, undermines his labour, dilutes his genius, embitters life.

'Here's a letter from your sister, and inspired by the admirable generosity and grandeur of her soul, against what's been agreed, I'll read you a paragraph: "Tell him to try and be happy and adapt to his new state. I'll keep him present in my memories but I understand how he needs to remake his life far from me. The gratitude I owe God and my husband compensates my grief at his absence. Dear Lord, I hope to see him one day when peace rules and embrace him in my arms as if he were still a child!"'

Basilio filed the letter in its folder and, after a pensive silence, invited him to get up and look through the window with him: a phalanx of energetic, able-bodied youths, supple and healthy-looking, marched by in warrior step to Veremundo's whistles and orders, one two, one two, right, left, half-turn, halt, attention and intone the 'Cara al sol' before they break ranks and cheerfully, noisily disperse in the barrack yard, in a spontaneous show of camaraderie to warm the cockles of his heart.

# DAAL

One had to study Felix's valuable collection of yellowing, faded postcards, images of a vanished era and a Medina bubbling with activity: the building works of the new city, broad boulevards and spindly palms; cafés favoured by officers and civil administrators of the Protectorate, the Gueliz Catholic church's inauguration in the presence of bishops and dignatories, the defunct Victoria Hotel's open-air restaurant. Or the sepia prints of the natives' unchanging, ritual life: side-alleys, sleepy figures, humble artisans, bygone trades. The Square, as ever, captured in its essential continuity and various disguises: the Post and Telegraph Office, brand new State Bank, hotels for Europeans, first omnibuses and Renault coupés, bustling horse-driven carriages, swift two-wheeled artefacts, object of shock and admiration. The Koutoubia's ethereal silhouette, its small tower, dome and golden spheres, viewed from the scrub behind, or from the panoramic terrace of the Hôtel de France. Then the helter-skelter of activity in its central space: food and drink stalls, agricultural labourers, their animals and tackle; fortune-tellers, water-sellers, quacks, nimble *gnaua* dancers, bystanders, perpetual nomads, *halca* gatherings, a protean, fertile versatility.

Amongst the shelves of postcards scrutinised in the small bookshop in Bab Ksur, one, in particular, had caught his eye: a close-up of a beggar, wrapped in a threadbare djellaba, seated with his staff on the ground. He was pushing his plate towards passers-by, only hinted at by their rustic moccasins, robust legs and heels. His beard seemed neat and tidy and he wore glasses – rather an anomaly in those days – it wasn't this really striking combination of detail which most disturbed him, but the plain outline of his nose and thin lips that were clearly European.

By chance might this be Eusebio?

Madame S. was quick to disabuse him of such wistful fantasies: Felix's last postcards dated at best from the early thirties: their author had died or given up his craft before the arrival of the Spaniards fleeing the war and setting themselves up in the old city and in Gueliz.

Surrounded by a group of her friends on the terrace of the Renaissance, he related his futile investigations in the macabre of Tanahaut: he'd easily found the tomb of the Gentile considered a saint, endowed with the gift of fertility and crowded out with barren women throughout the year; but after consulting and debating with numerous old folk, he'd reached the conclusion that it wasn't him. It was really the French quartermaster for Lyautey's troops, who'd lived in the village more than twenty years, companion at table and in bed to a charcoal burner, and a convert to Islam. His first name and surnames didn't match either, as he later checked in the archives: the man buried there forty years is a homonym – or a precursor? – of Jean Genet!

Then he climbed to the tiny cemeteries on the hills facing, visited hermitages of *marabouts* and whispering *zawiyas*, seeking the whereabouts of a friend buried in our land, the villagers said in their language, he's noble and good-hearted, gives out alms and offerings; some tried to take advantage of his largesse and pointed him down fantastical paths, knew the tomb of a *miliyi* or Melillan,

probably the deceased he was looking for. May God have
pity on his soul, he lived in an agricultural settlement in
Hauz and then next to the Oued Nfis reservoir, one of
the engineering gentlemen who built the dam and lived in
the cottages on the edge of the main road, a bachelor for
sure, and, what's more, he'd befriended a man from the Rif,
his grave was on the outskirts of the village, a simple pile
of whitewashed stones, he had wished it thus in his will, his
servant had died just before him and he had no heirs, the
grave had almost faded from view, but he remembered
the place perfectly and could drive him there if he so
desired.

Though sceptical, he agreed to climb to an abandoned
woodland cemetery on the cusp of a hill near the river gullies,
with magnificent views of the foothills and range of the
Atlas mountains, to the awesome majesty of the Toubkal.
His guide's well-rehearsed tale seemed coherent; but how
the devil could he prove it was the genuine grave?

Fear and doubts deepened, he said, by the fact that
another grave existed, identified a few kilometres from
Asni by another guide, a very holy *miliyi* or Melillan, still
the object of the prayers of the very elderly, a gentleman of
Gentile origins, also buried with his servant on a hilltop in
the neighbouring district.

He let himself be escorted yet again by half a dozen
villagers, attracted by his charitable veneer, to another
overgrown, weedy rural hideout, some twenty burial places
without inscriptions, the one he was looking for was, in
fact, the last one, beneath a fig-tree; here we called it the
one for the Melillan and his servant, may God have mercy
on their souls and keep them at His side.

'If I hear you aright, your poet resides in two different
graves,' Madame S. remarked with a touch of humour as he
finished the story.

'It wouldn't be at all surprising,' said one of the gathering who'd been listening silently. 'I would say it's even normal.'

Taking advantage of the attention his words drew, he extracted a visiting card from his pocket to reveal his credentials as a learned chronicler of the city.

'My name is Hamid and my initials figure on page 141 of the novel the only copy of which disappeared with the suitcase it was inside, which you and your friends, readers and colleagues in the Circle, are laboriously trying to piece together. As you see, I am a fictional character, only alluded to *en passant* and lacking any physical features!' (He burst out laughing.)

'In correspondence a few years ago with a colleague in a besieged city I mentioned this very topic: the multiplicity of tombs for a single *marabout* is my favourite theme! I suppose you are familiar with ancient Greek and Egyptian myths. Well, as far as the Maghreb is concerned, split personalities go back to the time when the saints appear. There is a tomb of Leyla Mimuna in al Garb, twenty kilometres from Souk al Arbaa, and another in the Taffert valley. Sidi Yahya Ben Yunis lies in the outskirts of Oujda but also on the perimeter of Algiers. According to legend, he enjoyed the miraculous gift of levitation and aerial flight, so this alternating of dwelling places is, I think, common and quite usual!'

He noted down everything he said in his journal and, when the waiters began to stack up the empty tables and they were forced to go their ways, he bid farewell to the gathering and returned by taxi to his cheap hotel in the neighbourhood of Riad Zitun. Before going to bed he added reflections of his own making to the leafy byways of legend. He thought of penning a detailed account of the survey to distribute on his return to the other readers in the Circle. Consequently, he was hugely astonished and upset when he confirmed, barely awake, that the ink in his diary had faded and its pages were white, desperately empty.

Was it a mischievous djinn's malicious doing or a felony committed by Madame S., in her desire to monopolise the dead man's memoirs and later write at the drop of a hat a mendacious, opportunistic biography?

# DTAL

*Sevilla, May 3, 1937, Second Triumphal Year*

*I've owed you this letter for several days, following on what*
*we agreed when, thanks to your valuable, fraternal assessment,*
*you and your colleagues — devoted body and soul to the Cause —*
*signed me off from the Medical Rehabilitation Centre. I wish you*
*could see my cure in person, the extent and depth of the change.*
*I remember the words you uttered with such resonance and splen-*
*did conviction that so greatly helped to rescue me from the pit*
*into which I was irrevocably sinking: 'Your admission into*
*Dr V.N.'s consultancy must mark a dividing line between the two*
*parts of your life, so that when you leave you will not only*
*have changed name but also your soul, a resurrected soul open*
*to the ideals of the Cause of Salvation.' I hope that when*
*you recognise this you'll feel proud of me, will measure the*
*progress I've made on the path you traced out for me. No need to*
*tell you how much I miss our conversations, your deeply felt*
*pity towards the sick, twisted being I then was, the incredible*
*care you showed my case the day my brother-in-law forged a new*
*identity for me and placed me in your hands, avoiding the exe-*
*cution I so deserved. I recreate you in my imagination smiling,*
*clad in your beautiful uniform, when I saw you on that last day,*
*in your blue shirt, arms aloft, your hair unkempt, ladling out*
*invaluable advice to me in that austere office presided over by the*

*photo of the Absent One where you used to receive me during my long catharsis.*

*Today has been unforgettable. An intensely blue firmament, not a wisp of cloud, one could say almost white it was so celestial. Absolute earth, absolute sky, set in a musical, theological, pure harmony. Our boys, parading magnificently, risen like ears of corn from the heroic, fertile heart of our great Nation: heads erect, striding powerfully, imbued with the sacrosanct values of the cleansing Crusade, their impassive miens hallowing the masterly lesson of destiny. These were moments of perfection: the will to Empire on the flags and to sacrifice in the hymns. I recalled the poem you recited to me, engraved for eternity on my memory:*

the blond hawks death do not fear
hovering, possessed by mystic love,
they seek her in dreams, their brows clear,
across the pain of ancient skies above

*The bellicose, lusty display, full of vital energies, of thousands upon thousands of youths breathed a singular luminosity into the atmosphere, a single, shared moral sense. The crowds gathered on the pavements also raised spirits. Next to the humble garments of the needy gleamed white linen suits and straw boaters; dark faces, tanned by the sun, mingled with German volunteers, infant eyes and titanic souls. Chest bemedalled, an officer on horseback rattled his spurs of war. Some youths of your age were also led by younger men from brotherhoods and associations. How stirring the brio and vigour of their squads, the sound of excited voices, the vision of unfurled flags, 'rose of time and pearl of evening stars, the youth of Spain!' I also remembered Veremundo, angelic meteorite of manly muscle, immaculately disciplined. I wish you were here by my side exulting in these splendid visions with me. What a breath of fullness, what life-enhancing grace swept my brow on that gentle summer's eve of jubilation!*

*Dear Basilio, I now understand everything you told me about the poetic essence of the dialectic of fist and pistol in defence of faith, nation and race. Yes, our rightful place is in the open air, on a serene night, gun on shoulder, and, on high, ever shining, the brightness of the constellations, the Milky Way, the Road to Santiago. As you say, we must eliminate all dregs of vulgar filth and resignation muddying our souls, of Jewish-masonic rabble-rousing and the spread of the virus of atheistic communism. I have also memorised the dictum of your psychiatrist friend who did his duty so well by me and put so much effort into my salvation: 'We must modify the cranium – the mentality – of Spaniards: that cranium democratised, liberalised, Frenchified and Europeanised by three centuries of cranial degeneration: and no better way to re-shape heads than to put them in the mould, the stubborn, sublimely fanatical mould of our berets.' If you see him, make sure you greet him and thank him on my behalf.*

*If only you'd seen the heroes of the Foreign Legion, noble, handsome, in serried ranks singing the Hymn! Inspiring in their vertical, rigid, vigilant stance. They marched by, straight-backed, dreaming, smiling, an impeccable shine on their boots and belts. Then I was present when they dispersed in festive mood, after the parade, to the bars of nymphs, wine and roses. You should have heard the loving tributes to the brides of our brave boys in the Legion!*

*You'll have noticed I've not said a word about the Mohammeds. They also marched with our boys, but I averted my gaze following your advice so as not to relapse into a past I hate and from which you, Veremundo and colleagues at the Centre saved me. I have also severed my old friendship with the Marquis of A\*\*\* , his syrupy lover and velvet pansies: his queenly flouncing and poses are a warning to keep my distance as a matter of elemental precaution. I don't understand how the new national patriotic order tolerates such attitudes so out of keeping with these ascetic, valiant times we live in.*

*I now go for coffee with a nurse from a traditionalist family and war-time godmother to two soldiers. We exchange sweet nothings and I try to court her. I read her poems from my recent flowering and others from the press of our Movement:*

With carnations from their hair,
twenty-five raven beauties
on your naked chests
yokes and arrows embroider

*The truth is I never get any further: the other day we were walking through the* parque de María Luisa *and one occasion she cuddled up to me, but I didn't know where to put my arms, so I carried on with my poetic flirtation and left her sad and disappointed in the entrance to the hospital.*

*And how about you? Where are you, what are you doing, who are you seeing, what sweet doves are you wooing? Tell me about your work as well, the new moment in your destiny. You don't know how I envy the air you breathe there.*

*I read, write a few pages, miss your immediate presence, recoup lost energies. I'm knocked over by reading the patriotic, powerfully racial poems in the recent anthology published by the Santaren bookshop in Valladolid. I sent one to the publisher but the book was already in press and it couldn't be included. I received, as consolation, José María Alfaro's magnificent poem:*

Like a bloody wind swirling
between cries that death decrees
Like the staff that passion cools
amid the fury of frenetic living.
Like a forest of light and a bow raised
above the thresholds life's initiating,
prince of Spain, you were in your pain,
redeemer, architect, angry mountain.

You saw the flag fly higher on parting
you grew two-fold in the light of your presence;
every angel knows your heartbeat sound
Fertile you made spring eternal
amid the clamour exalting your absence
everywhere will your memory resound.

*What extraordinary emotion and mastery! Pens like his will*
*soon raise our literature from the ashes.*

*Write to me, make sure you write, you know the happiness that*
*always, at every moment, I feel when I hear your voice, whether*
*in jest or serious, as it comes, straight from the heart.*

*Send a few lines to my sister and put her mind at ease, tell her*
*I'm well in my new skin and happy to dwell there, acclimatised*
*to this beautiful fertile space. In the present circumstances I prefer*
*not to show her any signs of life lest I inflame the wounds I*
*caused her when I was someone else.*

An illegible signature

# SECOND WEEK

# RAA

## The pasha's cook

The myths surrounding Madame S.'s cook just grew and grew from the day she took her on. The circumstances of their meeting, which some pious old folk were quick to dub initiatory, were an immediate subject for discussion and debate. Had she found her, as some suggested, on one of her wealthy widow's pleasure-seeking saunters among the tinkers' stalls where, seated in the sun behind an array of medicinal plants, sleek and billowing like a luminous storm cloud, she awaited a customer sent by providence? Opulently regal like a Mali queen, by way of introduction to her future benefactress, had she flourished the faded, blurred photograph of herself taken twenty years earlier in the company of the then powerful and feared pasha? Later, the version did the rounds, spread by Madame S.'s circle of friends, that the discovery was the fruit of a dream she'd had, in which she'd seen her step forward, imbued with diaphanous majesty, from amid the chanting of the blind and the tinkling of water-sellers' bells, in the helter-skelter confusion of the Square: apparently haloed by a supernatural light, sailing over the greasy, sticky tar as gracefully as a swan across glittering waters.

The woman herself neither endorsed nor denied any version: it had all been the work of God, she said. He guides our steps from on high, he decides our fate.

As her fame spread and her holy hand gained renown of
international dimensions (*trois étoiles* in the *Michelin Guide*),
the silence over her legendary past was sand-bagged and
defended like an impregnable fortress. Was she, as was
rumoured, the pasha's only trusted servant to the point that
he rejected all food and drink, however mouthwatering,
which she hadn't seasoned? Did he take her with him on
his journeys and visits to his castles in the Atlas mountains
in his retinue of courtiers, servants and *askaris* and appoint
her to select the maiden whose presence was to enliven
the cold nuptial bed? Had she accompanied him in an
aeroplane – yes, in an aeroplane! – to the metropolis, on
one of her master's displays of unswerving loyalty to the
now defunct colonial authorities? Who had instructed her
in the arcane mysteries of her incomparable art, which, once
honed in her possession she refused to share with
prebendaries, quarter-masters and galley-boys in the pasha's
household?

Her gradual eclipse over several years, after her master's
disgrace and death, remained shrouded in a haze as dark as
her skin and deepened the enigma surrounding her. The
gap between then and her transfiguring re-appearance in
Madame S.'s small but select restaurant encouraged all
manner of conjecture. Was she unjustly punished because
of her fidelity to her owner and had she experienced the
dire straits of extreme poverty? Like the ascetics in the
brotherhoods she frequented, did she pursue alone the
perfecting of her secret arts? Her much flagged virginity –
'nobody tickled my fancy' – was contradicted by none of
the elastic tongues agitating against her: she never
cohabited wth a male; none of the presumptuous rabble
around pretended they'd serviced her. 'I'll leave the world as
intact as I entered it,' she'd say in response to Madame S.'s
questions, in that ragged, second-hand French she so

lovingly cultivated. Single, without family or trusted friends, she lived down an alley by Bab Dukkala that she only left for the restaurant stoves or on visits to *zawiyas* and the tombs of the Medina's seven patrons, in search of a grace that they clearly granted her. If not, how could one explain the tasty, new recipes she continually invented?

Her date and place of birth were equally disputed: not even Madame S., when attempting to fill in the forms sent by the Administration, had managed to extract from her any distant approximations to the truth. 'Many, many years ago, my mother gave birth to me in the mountains, with nobody to help her.' 'How many?' She would smile mischievously and pretend to count on the fingers of her hands: not even a centipede could tot them up, she concluded, her grandmother'd come from Timbuctoo with Al-Mansour's army and her great-great-great grandma was Eve, of apple fame, only toasted and singed by the sun, like all African women. The figures inscribed on her identity card responded to no reality: 'Put I was born on the wayside,' she told the Civil Register bureaucrat in the presence of Madame S. 'Which way?' 'Anyone, one's as good as another. My mother begat me there, and that's an end to it.' 'Don't you remember which year?' She flashed her keyboard of gleaming white teeth: 'At a time when years didn't pass. When the French brought them in their suitcases along with street names and house numbers, I was already foot-loose and fancy free.'

Madame S. used to like telling this anecdote to her customers, when they fell over themselves to praise her cooking and it was time for tea, trays of cakes and croissants. Some celebrities wanted to see her and be photographed with her, but Madame S. apologised. The cook had been photographed once in her life, with the city's ex-pasha, and didn't want to see her image reproduced again. Neither would she agree to appear in the courtyard or to be paraded through the side rooms 'like a sheep sporting its Easter ribbon'. 'My saucepans know me well,' she repeated teasingly, 'they speak up for me better than my ugly face.'

When Madame S. reproached her sealed lips the day a minister from Paris came to her kitchen to congratulate her, she shrugged her shoulders with that dignity which so impressed those who knew her. 'He who's silent isn't silent,' she said, 'he only is silent who isn't silent.' This phrase, glossed by Madame S. at a dinner-party at the French Consulate's, sparked off a literary conversation among the city's academics, historians and male devotees. Some attributed the saying to Rabiaa, in love with Pure Love; others to Ibn Arabi, the Seal of the Saints. But how had an illiterate woman like her learned the phrase and how come she used it so opportunely, so naturally, so enigmatically?

From her very first days in the kitchen she decided to dot the i's and cross the t's: she was in charge in the kitchen and would brook no interference, not even from Madame S. 'You attend to the customers and the till and leave the stoves to me,' she told her. The secret of her art belonged to her: prying helpers who stuck their noses where they shouldn't were sacked without appeal. 'It's them or me,' she warned Madame S., 'what's cooking in the pots is my business.' Although Madame S. apparently submitted, she wasn't entirely resigned to defeat. The desire to control her secret, that mysterious ray of grace which like a gift from heaven transubstantiated all she touched, gnawed away at her, occasionally seemed to immerse her like the slow advance of high tide. Thanks to her employees' confidences, she knew the ingredients of the different dishes: but what was the exact mix and the precise moment things were cooked? Did those little bags hanging round her neck like scapularies or amulets hold the key to the mystery she jealously protected? Attempts to buy out her secret, with higher and higher offers, perished before her iron will. Why did she want all that money? She had more than enough with what her mistress paid her. Her expenses were minimal: alms, offerings to the saints, a bath in the hammam, embroidered slippers, comfortable clothes to wear. On her days off she went to a *zawiya* in the environs of the old town and prayed next to Sidi Rahal's tomb or Mulay Abdullah Ben Hsain's in Tamesleht.

Although the owner of the hammam she frequented, bribed by Madame S., passed on a sample of the content of the talismans filched while the cook was bathing, the sought-after ingredient – the philosopher's stone – turned out to be an anodyne powder, scattered over the dough in the basin it made no difference. The magic wasn't there, or else it had slipped between her fingers. Was the cook's sudden stand a presentiment, or an intuition of that unacceptable interference? Her 'I'm sorry, I'm on strike today' couldn't have come at a worse moment: the day a delegation of posh customers arrived from Paris to sample her cooking! Madame S. had rushed *en catastrophe* to Bab Dukkala to beg her to come, but the cook stuck to her guns, like the saints and hermits she worshipped on their fasts: her grace had deserted her, she must buy a bus ticket to go to Mulay Brahim. God would illumine the replacement chosen to satisfy the palates of the noble French gentlemen! But there was no such illumination and Madame S. swallowed the humiliation of serving up a fake banquet: half a dozen specialities of the house in a sorry, tasteless state. The three stars in the Guide went pale or hid behind a dark cloud. Happily, nobody divulged the unfortunate twist of fate and the gourmet present preferred to act the innocent. After all, he said, as he took his leave from the wake, like any footballer or torero, everyone has their off days.

When the cook returned and took possession of her stoves, the good spirit or hand of the saint blessed the place anew. Madame S. breathed a mixture of relief and resignation. By trying to sniff out the secrets didn't she run the risk of repeating the story of the goose and the golden eggs? Better leave things as they were and enjoy her cook's portentous grace, her ever refreshed inventiveness, her clientele's unfailing satisfaction. The restaurant's reputation spread and reservations for the select few tables had to be made several weeks in advance. Madame S. had no favourites: you strictly waited your turn, only those with forethought, those on the list, had right of entry. Whether it was a customer in a hurry or last minute on spec, or the US ambassador or His Majesty's right-hand man. She was sorry, next time they should take the simple precaution of calling her and agreeing a date. She was proud of the implacable logic of rules that flattered her vanity.

However, a vague anguish gnawed away. What would happen the day her cook – age unknown, but getting on in years – should fall ill, retire, could no longer be relied on? Should she resign herself to the collapse and demise of her establishment and not attempt somehow to predict the future and ensure a succession? Very cautiously she broached the subject with the person concerned: the need to hand on the secrets for fear they'd be lost, to reveal to a person of trust the arcane matter she guarded so jealously. If the king oversaw the education of the heir who was to prolong the glories of the dynasty, why couldn't she follow his wise example and advise and instruct an assistant of her choosing? She listened in silence, fanning herself like a serene *duenna* listening to her ladies-in-waiting's empty chatter, responded in silence or let drop one of her pearls of wisdom:

'The king is king and disposes of the wealth and people of his kingdom. My business is small fry.' Then, pointing to the saucepans and utensils lined up on shelves and racks, she added, much to Madame S.'s surprise and embarrassment: 'Look at the inanimate objects, at all the pots and pans and hear their permanent glorification of God.'

She was really worried by her cook's health. For some time she'd been less nifty than usual, displayed signs of exhaustion. She was as spirited as ever but occasionally, in the run up to lunch or dinner, she would slump on a stool and just supervise with half an eye the labours of her kitchen boys and girls. Visits to the saints she worshipped and potions from a reputable faith-healer in Mukef seemed to make no impact. It's the cold, she said quite simply, God gives us our health and takes it away; the day it pleases him he'll restore it. Nevertheless, she let Madame S.'s chauffeur drive her home, and climbed the steep steps to her burrow with increasing difficulty.

The 'cold' which, according to her, was plaguing her couldn't explain the pain and sudden loss of weight. The doctors at the General Hospital who examined her, X-rayed her uncovered bosom in the dark, and then explained to her it was a serious illness requiring long, difficult treatment. She didn't understand their coagulated jargon and only when the nurse, a neighbour of hers from Bab Dukkala, heard her prayers and sighs, told her 'nobody can escape their destiny', in order to calm her down, did she recover her peace of mind. She must heed her and come regularly to the hospital: there she'd receive some invisible rays brought by doctor gentlemen from France and, God willing, would be back in good health.

The treatment – and subsequent hospitalisation – cost an arm and a leg and the cook knew she couldn't foot the bill. Madame S. had temporarily shut the restaurant 'for repairs' and immediately came to the rescue. She'd pay the costs of doctors, medicine, radiotherapy and a single room on one condition: she must reveal her secrets. Exhausted by the doctors' savage cure and the sickness eating into her, the cook yielded. She'd reveal them one by one, in writing, as long as her illness went on. Madame S. should appear once a week with a sage from her favourite *zawiya* and she'd dictate into his ear the hidden grace of each dish. In French? asked Madame S. No, in my language. When we finish, get a sworn translator and he'll throw some light on my words. Madame S. nodded and sought out her cook's friendly sage. As agreed, the patient showed him the contents of her lucky charms, revealed their secrets. But, to maintain their power and not go awry, they had to be stowed safely in the holy man's inlaid cask. The sage, a devotee of Sidi Mehdi, would protect them with his grace.

The cook wasted away daily and her secrets, carefully captured in limpid calligraphy, were placed like pearls in the saint's chest for safe-keeping. 'Don't try to find them out before I die,' she warned her benefactress, 'the last, the most recondite remains. Without that, all I've revealed is worthless and you'd be wasting your time and money on empty husks.'

Was it a ruse to extend her treatment and be regally attended by the nurses and doctors in the hospital? Madame S.'s compatriots, always suspicious of the natives, thought it so and forewarned her against deception. What was that Secret of Secrets which nobody could snatch from her mouth? Rather than let herself be bamboozled and obey her instructions to the letter, she must get hold of the recipes kept by the sage, translate them as God willed from incomprehensible squiggles to plain language and check out their miraculous properties.

Madame S. was all at sea: desperate to possess the secrets, she feared the cook's warnings and the risk of spoiling everything through impatient haste. However, the doctors in the General Hospital played along: her employee was on the way out, only their intensive care was keeping her alive, she'd pass away in a matter of days, if not hours. One question tormented her: pallid, drugged by painkillers, unable even to emit a miserable whimper, how could she reveal the final secret to the sage?

In the end, anxiety overcame prudence: she ran to the sage's house, with gifts and guile obtained the little packets of secrets and handed them to the sworn translator who had always served her family. Come by this afternoon, he said, everything will be done before darkness falls.

Madame S.'s friends and relatives later narrated the scene in get-togethers and cafés frequented by Europeans: the *trujaman* handed her the literal translation of the secrets revealed in a single sentence, repeated according to circumstance, seven, thirty-three, forty, ninety-nine times, not one more or less. Madame S. read hurriedly, deeply despondent, incredulous.

'He who seeks the secret outside himself, loses himself and loses his secret.'

'Was that all?', she managed to stammer.

'Yes, that's it.'

'And the recipes?'

'This is her only secret!'

Madame S. had a fainting fit that lasted days. And so was unable to accompany the usual weepers from Bab Dukkala and be at her cook's funeral. After the forty days' mourning, she re-opened the restaurant and stood over her stoves. The food was most delicious and her customers asked her as usual to congratulate the authoress of such exquisite flavours. Madame S. promised she would.

That was how the pasha's cook survived in subtle state and became a living legend. Only Madame S. knows of her absence and punctually every Friday meditates quietly before her tomb.

# ZAAY

In the present climate of fanatical hysteria and persecution, I'm forced to be extremely cautious, monitor my slightest word or gesture, fearful that any slip or unpremeditated sentence might burden me with the intolerable humiliation of prison or, at best, the traumatic experience of another bout of rehabilitation. I strive constantly to see myself from someone else's point of view, say, one of the possible trusties keeping an eye on me, waiting for the first careless moment to go and tell all to the guardians of the new moral, political regime. The continual straining to display emotions I don't feel and to silence those driven by strength of desire is in the end exhausting and corrosive. Silencing my feelings and ideas, hiding my face beneath a mask of conventional, self-righteous thought sometimes seems a worse punishment than a *paseo* or the firing squad. Death is merciful compared to this ceaseless, heavy vigilance.

I remember the day when, thanks to Basilio's intervention, I recovered my furniture and padlocked trunks from my old lair in Cádiz – so many pleasant, memorable associations – the notion of all that treasure filled me with panic: compromising letters, photos carrying sentences beyond appeal, poems worthy of the dungeon, drawings ripe for the Inquisition. After carefully closing behind me the door and windows to my new flat, I performed a secret *auto-da-fé*, delivered to the flames all that might make me in turn fuel for the bonfire.

A manuscript of a sonnet by Lorca, letters from Luis Cernuda, postcards from Manolo and Concha, from friends executed by the Soul-Saving Crusade or now exiled somewhere in the world. Disappeared thus, reduced forever to ash and smoke.

Meticulously assembled from student days, my library suffered the same fate. What books could I spare if most of their authors were labelled as Reds and atheists, except those who'd taken a cure and now donned the Falange's beret and shirt? Burn the lot! I burnt them one by one to avoid attracting the attention of an ever-watchful neighbourhood, I soon noticed, spying on my every word and deed. One night, I ventured into the street with a bag of incriminating evidence and, shaking with fright, threw it into the river. I'd bought myself some records of military marches and hymns and flung my window wide-open, and put them on the old gramophone pretending to enjoy non-stop the 'Cara al sol' and 'Oriamendi'.

To the world outside, in cafés or the Press and Propaganda Offices where I presented myself with Veremundo and Basilio's letters of introduction, I commented with equal doses of enthusiasm on the content of war dispatches, the ever victorious offensives against the traitors to the Fatherland. I offered them poems and articles, my diatribes against the red peril and dithyrambs to the Crusade, yet never managed to dispel the atmosphere of suspicion around me. The more tangible it became, the greater my efforts to maintain my conversion, my splendid normality.

In official waiting-rooms and chambers, I never failed to court secretaries and try to be seen with them in public places. I invented absent girlfriends. One afternoon I invited home a boss from Social Services, stood beside her on my

balcony, made sure the whole block saw us. Somebody had
spread rumours about me and my past: my immediate
neighbours spied on me, even opened their doors if some
errand-boy or door-to-door salesman rang my bell,
reminding me all the time of my precarious status in an era
of vertical salutes and imperial language when the slightest
dissension or anomalous behaviour was judged to be
subversive and worthy of punishment.

(A few steps from my front door, almost on the corner
of Sierpes, was a bevy of activists, half a dozen war widows
who, on seeing me, broke off their sewing and gossiped
about my abnormal bachelor state and doubtful loyalty to
the Movement. Although I usually wore the blue shirt with
yoke and arrows and trumpeted skywards my devotion to
the memory of José Antonio, nothing disarmed their wary
attitude and heavy-handed condemnations.)

Any inhabitant of that city of a thousand and one eyes
could be my executioner. I remember the day when
hearing someone whisper my old name, my heart missed a
beat and I almost fainted from fright. But it wasn't a grass
or an MSB agent, only an ex-journalist camouflaged like
me, a regular in the theatrical circles frequented by
Federico, whom he hadn't seen since his ill-destined trip to
Melilla and the cataclysmic Uprising. He said 'Glad to
know you're alive' and immediately hurried on, turned
down the first side-street and quickly disappeared amid the
traffic.

Eusebio's brusque forays into my life, together with the
emotion and panic they brought, injected a precious blast
of oxygen into the daily asphyxia: that unequal fight against
an infinitely headed hydra, a savage universal suffrage of
thugs guarded by an invisible cohort of spies. Despite my
protests of normality and adherence to the new order,
reiterated in letters I sent to Basilio, my 'cure' was fake: the

old demons buried in my deepest self palpitated with life, suddenly surfaced from stagnant waters with blind, irrepressible violence.

One night, after leaving an assembly at the Provincial Headquarters for Press and Propaganda, while walking home across the deserted gardens of the 1929 Exhibition, I spotted in the shadows the presence of a sturdy, horny, handle-bar moustachioed trooper from the Regulars. Without hesitation I followed him into the thick undergrowth, fell to my knees as he unbuttoned and offered me his staff of life: 'official weapon of a nefast artillery'. Impossible to describe the fullness of my emotion, the symbiosis of fear and pleasure, trembling genuflection between his knees, my fevered lips, my oscillating head – still wearing my beret! – round his thick, insurgent shaft. I've never lived nor will ever re-live such a moment. The clandestine nature of the act, the danger I ran, the ephemeral after-darkness of the encounter precipitated the intensity of enjoyment down a slope, to depths unattainable in less tough times. Hours later as I recalled the episode in my miserable Falange enclosure, Cernuda's diamantine verses, which my alter ego had read and re-read years ago, rushed to my memory . The poem's succinct truth stunned me: a spark from those pleasures could destroy the opaqueness of the world with its brilliance.

Framed by its inquisitional triangle, hanging atop the Giralda in place of the thin slice of crescent moon, had God's implacable Eye registered the body-blowing event?

# SEEN

A story-line never on line or a leisurely way of beating about the bush: that's what I think of the tale told this night. A digression, with literary pretensions, diverting us fom the search for Eusebio, the true aim of our Circle and its weekly meetings in this delightfully cultivated garden.

My fellow readers' exaggerated credulity in respect of Madame S. of the routinely concealed surname, has led us astray at a crossroads of fake foliage and futile ramifications. Who indeed was that famous pasha's cook to whom, my colleague devoted, not without talent, page after page? A woman from Ouarzazat who never served El Glaui, whose succulent but ordinary stews kept the restaurant's tourist clientele happy thanks to the scenario and myths carefully contrived by her boss, very well in, that's for sure, with the pseudo-gourmets sent by the *Michelin* guide to star or unstar the Marrakesh sky!

Incurable yarn-spinner that Madame Dupont, the family name under which she disembarked in the port of Casablanca as a youngster, later known as Caroline in the brothels she ruled over and where she managed to amass a considerable fortune! She married, or so she reckoned, a certain Colonel Saint Saëns, a relative, naturally, of the famous composer, a husband whose widow she apparently became a few months later.

But let's take one step at a time. The nucleus of French survivors from the last days of the Protectorate still remember her over-the-top face-paint and procuress ways before she stopped slumming it and acquired a civilised, worthy patina. She longed to rival Manon Lescaut and Marguerite Gautier, women who, by hearsay, not through her reading, she imitated. She regularly attended musical and literary soirées, absorbed like a sponge the audience's comments, the words and names quoted by almost invariably mediocre lecturers. Although initially she mistook Descartes for Sartre and Miró for a friend of Velázquez's, her knowledge became more sophisticated, she found friends among the Marrakshi fond of the arts and literature and gradually forged herself in young people's eyes a halo that, if it wasn't exactly intellectual, at least made her an enlightened *grande dame*, a kind of Madame Verdurin for the unsuspecting and naive.

Via a reputable historian of the city, I befriended a Moroccan, a retired civil servant from the colonial administration, an acerbic septagenarian, a no-holds-barred raconteur whose quicksilver tongue rattled with the wit and mimicry of the unforgettable Barrault.

'Oh, Madame Caroline!' he sighed. 'You should have seen her in the good old days! She was known and respected from the French High Commissioner down to the lowliest legionary. She became as well-known in military brothels as de Gaulle!'

He had recourse to her pleasant services in Khenifra, at a time when he presided over the province's forests and her benign if ruthless hand governed the knocking-shop on the perimeter of the Foreign Legion's airy, well-equipped barracks. Everybody had passed through. Madame Caroline still kept a precious possession, the Livre d'Or with the flourishes of the military chiefs whose presence honoured her noble House. The signature to beat all signatures, the pearl of pearls, was a dedication from the High Commissioner himself, *oui, du général Guillaume*! Although now a respectable widow, Madame Saint Saëns's cheeky pride got the better of her and she showed it to him: '*J'aime les chevaux, j'aime les femmes, j'aime le couscous de notre chère Caroline.*' In her Gueliz flat, packed with furniture and would-be family mementoes, she would wait a few seconds to gauge the impact of the text, as if they were original lines from Cervantes or Shakespeare. 'I know he's not highly regarded in Morocco because of his role in removing the sultan, but he was a perfect gentleman, extremely polite and generous towards the ladies.'

Madame Saint Saëns's brand-new position and patchwork culture won her the devotion of the new generations but soon fell apart when she was distracted or under the influence of liqueurs or cordials. One afternoon when she summoned him to her salon, all chatty and bright-eyed, on the pretext of seeking his advice as to which of the latest books published in France to purchase, they ended up in a duet evoking the era of her hospitable mansion in Khenifra and his glorious exploits in battle. The ex-go-between's crude, flowery language, full of quasi-Rabelaisian expressions and turns of phrase, is difficult to adapt, so I had recourse – o woe is me the *tradittore*! – to a bunk-up from the one and only Moll from Andalucia.

'Big-hearted Madame Caroline, a big-hearted woman, expert number-cruncher endowed with innate commercial and common sense! She organised a cat-house with fifty or so wards, for all tastes, a confetti of nationalities, which he knew well for he frequented them often, being young and single, a respite from the crushing solitude and silence of his small European-style villa tucked away in the woods. She'd enforced a rigid hierarchy of values in line with the military system with which she cohabited: illiterate Berber peasants for the rank and file; the better-educated and brightest of them for sergeants, aides-de-camp and corporals; Jewish and Spanish women for captains and lieutenants; good-looking but most daring French women, the exclusive domain of the top brass. A general's visit was greeted with music and a round of *yuyus*!

'Everything ran like clockwork and Madame Caroline sprinkled wordly-wise advice over those she affectionately called her daughters. They should put every honourable effort into satisfying the customers and never fall in love with the riff-raff who would try to trick them with their lying lip in order to get a free lay. If it's a quickie, keep it plain and simple; if it's demanding and dirty, make it every way it turns them on, none of the in-your-face stuff from that Valencian wench with her "we fuck *à la española*: if you want shit, get yourself a Parisienne!". You must learn to sway and shimmy, gyrate and shake your breasts, to prepare the terrain for amorous jousts with captains and lieutenants. As for the country lads, firm-bellied and hard-shafted, horny thrusters, hitting bullseye and sending you to heaven, watch out! Enjoy!, but don't forget the scant pay-off and faint regard for extras. As for the worn-out or ageing officer, slow to stiffen and never bringing joy, caress and indulge till he stands to attention and pretend to savour the droplets of his tiny spurt of jism as if it were a fount of rich, thick honey. Keep an eye out before you entertain or slot in a member!: see whether it's caught a "cold" as the Berbers say, or shows signs of a visit from the blessed Saint Gonorrhoea. Demand sheaths be used and, if you fall ill, tell me right away. My darlings, I'll make sure they attend to you, like doughty fighters, in the military hospital so that, safe and sound, you can resume your meritorious labours for Fatherland and Foreign Legion! I don't want you to leave here one day sick or needy! Look after your earnings and estate, so you can retire decorously and marry an honest, well-heeled husband. What could give me greater pleasure than to come to one of my daughters' country wedding, the fun and frolicks at the banquets with roast lamb, dancing and *jaimas*, after years of loyal toil on the bed of all battles, on behalf of the public good and the Army! One day I too will retire from the field and expect to leave head held high, with honour and all manner of recognition, after doing my social duty!'

That was more or less the forestry engineer's speech on the confidences from his hostess in her chambers adorned with the mirrors, jugs and bric-à-brac described by Dumas in his *Lady of the Camelias*. By the end, he'd downed his two fingers of fiery plum liqueur, probably from Denmark or Germany, and your learned, lettered Madame S., two and a half bottles of her beloved Marie Brizard!

# SHEEN

'What a sight for sore eyes! What a surprise! That's what you call mistaking baskets for cabbages, or, to add the fruit of my wit to our treasury of proverbs, lofty imperial eagles for chattery, pansied parakeets.'

(Who was that fellow, all grinning yellow teeth and leathery lips, smothering him in fawning, festive familiarity?)

'Just imagine, I came to say hello to an old comrade, one of Queipo's brothers-in-arms and on-the-town who lives in the building next door, I get the wrong front entrance and run into you!, a turn-up for the books! Well, every cloud has its silver lining, I'm pleased to introduce myself and, if I'm not in the way or upsetting your domestic routine, to chin-wag about friends we hold in common.'

(The guy wore a creased white suit dappled with cigarette burns and stains, sported the regulation pencil moustache and in his lapel, the emblems of the Crusade; uninvited, he crossed the threshold, sniffed the flat like a bloodhound and his bleary, bulging eyes were a picture, as they seemed to record every detail of wall and furniture.)

'I'm Cándido Suárez, don't you recognise me? we bumped into each other a couple of times in the corridors or on the stairs of the Headquarters of the Movement when collecting our orders or handing in poems or articles, for

I, too, modestly court the muses, feel an urge to versify, exactly so, uplifted by our glorious, national epic, a few months ago I published an "Ode to José Antonio" and some sonnets to our Caudillo, the Saviour of the West, if you don't know them I'll get you a copy from the office, of course not aspiring to reach the sublime peaks of a Pemán or the grandeur of a Luys Santamarina, but they're sincere, straight from the heart, on the sleeve, in these times rent with anxiety if full of hope, we must pile in, lend a hand, join forces against the red, atheist hordes, fight for a pure, regenerated Spain, shed the horrible dead weight of the past, the filthy tide of Republican rabble.'

(Now perched on the canvas chair, cigarette hanging from the corner of his lip.)

'Got an ashtray?, ah, you don't smoke?, a nasty mannish habit, my mother used to say, but what one can do? when one gets the habit, no way one can stop, any saucer or glass will do the trick, don't want to spoil your lovely soft rug with my blessed butts, *c'est la vie*, can't function without my dose of nicotine, particularly when I'm writing articles or, if the gods are good and I'm counting my syllables.'

(The stranger – had they really bumped into each other down the corridors of Headquarters? he had no recollection – looked him straight in the eye, had taken his Press card and Movement membership card from his wallet and was waving them between brown-stained fingers like a football referee.)

'I've been wanting to chat and exchange ideas with you for a while, something perfectly normal between colleagues, united by love for the same ideal, for the Fatherland, don't you think?, certainly the first time I saw you, after a mass of remembrance for the Absent One, I mistook you for someone I'd known by sight years earlier, someone also fond of poetry and a little bit of this and that

that's not to the point, one of these godless, mentally perverted clones from the Liberal Education outfit in Madrid, but I was soon put right when I saw you had a different name and weren't from Cádiz like him but from the Canary Islands, curious as I am – goes with the trade – I consulted the register to make sure and saw you were born in Las Palmas.'

'Well
(his voice trembled and he strove to be concise)
a few kilometres from Arucas.'

'Arucas? you're kidding! I was only there last week, not as a tourist naturally, but for indoctrination, if I'd had an inkling I'd have presented my respects to your family.'

'I've no family left. My parents died when I was a child and my grandfather, may he rest in peace, sent me to study with the Jesuits in Málaga.'

'Oh, that accounts for the lack of a Canary Island accent, I was just going to mention that and you took the words out of my mouth.'

(The intruder sprawled back over the seemingly conquered territory of the sofa, took another stinky cigarette out of his jacket pocket, lit it with his lighter, peered at the portraits of Franco and José Antonio, and the miniature nationalist flag hoisted ostentatiously between the pens and paperweights on his desk.)

'Forgive my being so rude, I haven't asked after your good lady.'

'I'm a bachelor.'

(There was a brief, pregnant silence.)

'Oh, a bachelor!, that has its drawbacks and its advantages, my wife works as a nurse in the military hospital in Jerez, and that allows me to go on the binge from time to time, to sow a few wild oats!'

(Was he going to invite him to a night on the town, with

spliced, high-octane wines, a bevy of doxies in awe of belts
and pistols, skirts a flutter, showing all their wares, 'their
hidden treasures like currency on the blink'.)

(There was no invite to binge, no date with the legionary
bard, only a curt, unexpected question.)

'Are you a friend of Comrade Basilio?'

'Yes, I am. Why?'

'Somebody mentioned it in the office.'

'More than a friend, a brother, he helped me at a critical
time, a noble, courageous individual, like all those constructing the new Spain.'

(Was his riposte convincing? The Movement's poet-
journalist cleared his throat, he too had had occasion to
see him, he said, in his Army medical consultant's office,
Veremundo as well and their able-bodied centurions,
models of military discipline, impeccably turned-out, goose-
stepping parades, devotion to our leader, hymns to the
Falange, he broke off mid-stream as if disturbed by fleeting
thoughts, sombre cloudlets scudding across the peaceful
firmament, an expression of wily innocence and cunning
curiosity.)

'Have you heard from him of late?'

(His bulbous, black-headed face suddenly seemed to
darken.)

'We write regularly. I got a postcard from him a couple
of weeks ago.'

'Did he say anything?'

'Anything about what?'

'Apparently he's run into problems, nasty rumours about
him and his group, I thought he might have confided the
tight scrape he's in, well, some officers have denounced him.'

'Not an inkling about any of this.'

(Had he responded to his innuendo with the necessary
sang-froid?)

'Oh, it's probably envy, people exaggerate, go over the top out of pure bitchiness.'

(He was now looking at him like an inspector of police.)

'Funny, you look worried.'

'I can't believe an idealist like Comrade Basilio . . .'

(His voice went hoarse.)

'Don't get alarmed, perhaps it's not serious, but it was my duty as a friend to inform you.'

(He cleared his throat.)

'From now on, watch your step.'

(Was he aware of his identity? Hadn't they destroyed all his previous documentation at the Military Rehabilitation Centre?)

'Basilio has his weak points, well, you know as well as I do which way his compass swings, his choreography of Seraphic adolescents is the talk of the town.'

(The stranger slapped the ash off his trousers, his smile congealed in a leer.)

'If you're summoned, speak your mind, I only came to give you some advice, we're at war and the enemy infiltrates the most surprising crannies, your duty is to collaborate with us, to help us unmask him by making a strong statement.'

# SAAD

## A thousand nights less one

From the terrace-roof of his little house in the Casbah, in
the hours Eusebio read and meditated under the friendly
rays of the morning sun, he was exhilarated by the vision
of the *mechouar*'s ochre walls, the park's palm and olive
trees, the rocky reaches of the gleaming, bronzed Atlas
mountains. Closer to hand, inside the fortified empty
precinct where sultans of old heard their subjects' woes and
worries, his attention was fleetingly caught by the
gardener's lean silhouette hidden by flower beds and shaped
hedges from all eyes but his own. This furtive presence,
sheltered by the sweet warmth of his hideaway, melded
harmoniously with the tableau, added a cordial touch to
the wintry repose he sought. Occasionally, disturbed by the
wail of sirens escorting some dignitary, he instinctively
looked up at the haven where the boy was dreaming to find
him in a raking and pruning dance routine, absorbed in
feigned labour and momentary zeal while the cortège of
cars zoomed across the esplanade carrying the cream of the
realm beneath the arches of the *mechouar*. The silent
connivance uniting them strengthened in the interludes
between reading: minutes after the brusque interruption, in
another pause between intermittent onslaughts on his
book, he spotted him crouching down again with his pipe
of kef, far, very far from the madding crowd. The youth had

also sensed the bond of complicity, the approving recognition of his sorties on the part of that foreigner-reader: they watched one another at a distance, separated by the pond whence rose the frogs' monotonous croak, and returned to their respective bliss, mutually comforted by silent acquiescence and affinity.

His name was Boujmaa, said the concierge of the little house where he resided after the death of his faithful friend for life: he'd come from the countryside some months ago and had no friends or relatives in the city. Poorly dressed and shod, wearing an elfin woolly hat, he nevertheless seemed to enjoy that poorly paid, menial job. Kef was his only consolation and he smoked it leisurely, before and after opening his luncheon cornet of peanuts or sweetcorn and saying his ritual prayers prostrate towards the *qibla*.

One morning he looked for him and, though he patiently inspected the flower beds and pots near the palace, he could see him nowhere. But any anxiety in respect of his absence lasted less than a day. The old man serving him dinner, informed him, half jealous, half upset, of the surprising news: Boujmaa had got married!

What? When? And, in particular, to whom?

On the occasion of the birth, marriage and anniversary of one of his daughters, a blue-blooded prince had decided to marry and magnanimously endow one of his most faithful servants as a reward for services given!

What's this got to do with Boujmaa?

Following the royal's instructions, members of his retinue trawled the palace environs for likely candidates and, one way or another, paths led his way.

Who had told that incredible story?

Incredible? No, it was for real! He'd seen him with his own eyes: Boujmaa taken to the tailor's and the hairdresser's in a black limousine, sleek, silent, long as a crocodile! Once

he was spruced up and ready, they'd take him to his village
to collect his family.

His betrothed . . .

He wouldn't meet her till the ceremony. Who knows
whether she'd be pretty . . .

And if she weren't?

So what? Once he was in the dynast's service, there'd be
no shortage of opportunities to find another . . .

He fell asleep gratifyingly at peace with himself. Boujmaa
cleaned up and in a smart suit! Escorted in a Mercedes to the
palace! Married to the maid of a generous ruler into
the bargain!

Wasn't that perhaps the dream he'd secretly cherished in
his benign hideaway while he took the pipe from his sock
and lit his pipe of kef?

He returned to his terrace readings mingled with relaxing
pauses, when he surveyed the jagged outline of the
mountains, the graceful plumes of the palm trees, the
crenelated walls of the *mechouar*. A pair of storks had built
their nest on the neighbouring mansion's slender tower. He
watched them glide majestically and bid farewell to each
other in the air: one left for the olive grove to get food and
the other came back to the look-out point to see to her
offspring. In the grounds and gardens outside the palace,
brightened by the myriad colours of the guards and
sentinels' turbans and berets, the servants watered pots of
roses and sheared privet hedges. After a few hours
wandering through the world of Ibn Arabi, he raised his
head, responding to a premonition, and directed his gaze
to the spot where his accomplice used to crouch: there was
Boujmaa!

He rushed to see the old man. Why the devil had he
lied? What was the boy doing in the garden, with his frayed
djellaba and pointed, woolly hat? At this moment shouldn't

he be with his betrothed, enjoying the gift of an all-expenses-paid wedding?

Version according to Boujmaa: the dynast's cook, who was looking for a husband, was old, no, ancient, seventy-years plus, had been tarted up to conceal her wrinkled hide, but he caught a glimpse, though the encounter was almost in the dark, and almost died of fright, for God's sake, how could he take as spouse a toothless woman with one foot in the grave? Might as well marry his grandma! So he took his leave there and then and gave the dynast his presents back.

In fact, the concierge sarcastically commented after gathering up different versions of the episode in a punctilious tour of the neighbourhood, things hadn't turned out in tune with Boujmaa's tale. She'd rejected him. They'd looked for three candidates for her to choose from and she'd opted for someone else. The old age and toothlessness he'd invented to hide his disappointment and hurt pride.

He saw him back in his hideaway, on one of his frequent pauses from the daily tedium of work, in threadbare djellaba and elfin hat, ruminating, smoking, ritually praying. Everything had apparently been a dream: betrothed, presents, Mercedes, visit to the tailor and hairdresser, failed encounter in the palace. They looked knowingly at each other and, as before, he took his pipe from his sock, inhaled a few puffs of kef, levitated on his rug, happy and weightless.

As far as Eusebio's old servant had been able to ascertain, nobody asked Boujmaa to return his wedding suit and, trusting to his lucky star, he was keeping it in his cupboard, carefully draped over a hanger, for better days.

# DAAD

## Secret Report by the MSB to the Military Government in Granada dated May 1937

In response to the written complaint filed by several officers of the Provincial Junta of the Movement concerning alleged divisive activities carried out by a nucleus of comrades from the National Syndicalist Movement, supporters of the Hedilla theses and opposed to Unification, the Chief of Police issued the necessary orders to the general responsible from the Military Special Branch to intensify security investigations around these comrades, captained by Basilio★★★ and Veremundo★★★, whose influence seems to extend to other cadres within the Falange Political Training School as well as to several dozen youths enrolled there.

As a result of these preventive police enquiries, coordinated by Angel Posada García, head of the 'Martyrs of Aragón' group, comprising nine inspectors, its members have managed to assemble a panoply of evidence partly confirming the afore-mentioned accusations and pointing up the existence of behaviours and practices contrary to nature and moral order.

This is a written résumé of their conclusions.

Behind a façade of unbesmirched loyalty to the ideals of José Antonio Primo de Rivera, Onésimo Redondo and Ramiro Ledesma, the above comrades avoid publicly all manifestation of adherence to the Caudillo of Spain and Generalísimo of her Armies, as well as to the 19th April Decree of Unification. Their theory classes focus on the social and political programmes of those Martyrs, emphasising their anti-bourgeois, revolutionary content. 'If José Antonio were alive, everything would have been different,' Basilio said according to one eye-witness. 'He wanted no truck with the monarchists now embedded in our ranks or with that gang of landowners applauding us in the belief we will restore their lands and privileges to them and, as the Protomartyr used to say, become the Shock Troops of Reaction, charged with saving their bacon and safeguarding their slumbers in casino armchairs and on barren estates.' Later, in another private meeting of the group's ring-leaders, Comrade Veremundo described the unifying Decree of 19th April and the subsequent arrest and imprisonment of Hedilla as 'a coup d'état and crime crying out to heaven'. A separate sheet carries a detailed list of all the private and public expressions of a similar political character, with furtive allusions to the Caudillo and an alleged betrayal of the ideals of José Antonio.

The investigations into these comrades' past have been less fruitful: the documentation referring to Veremundo's entry into the National Syndicalist Youth in 1933, where one would find references to his political past and ideological evolution drawn up by the man himself, are unfortunately in the Red Zone and a closed book to us; Basilio's is thin on the ground. According to reports commissioned by the Head of the State Archives and the Information Centre of the Falange, a few days ago, he came in person with an armed escort to access the same and suppress them. One of our agents notes how the biographical note with his request to join the Falange in 1934 disclosed previous contacts with the CNT. If this were true, it would supply our Services an invaluable lead inasmuch as they would clarify the possible existence of clandestine links between this comrade and ex-believers on the other side. Unfortunately, to this day there is no valid, legal proof of such an assumption.

In respect of the other point we alluded to, the verified facts are devastatingly conclusive: Comrades Basilio and Veremundo, like their trusty collaborators, shamelessly deliver themselves up to unnatural acts and practices with diverse members of the youthful phalanx they are indoctrinating. So-called nighttime political orientation meetings are in fact a cover for courses in sexual perversion where youths are incited to perform disgusting touchings-up described by Comrade Basilio as 'rites of passage into manhood'. The revelations of one participant who, intimidated by his superiors in rank, didn't dare denounce what happened, shows the wretched ignominy of private and collective scenes in which, through fallacious evocations of Greek and German myths, both comrades perverted minors and inducted them into sodomy and other aberrations too repugnant to mention. Some snaps, apparently taken by Basilio, catch two actors in those filthy orgies in a position whose criminal, anti-natural character is beyond doubt.

In a word: the investigations carried out by the Special Branch at several points endorse submissions presented to the Provincial Junta of the Movement concerning the fractionist tendencies of the afore-mentioned group of comrades and offer irrefutable eye-witness proof of the sexual deviations of those denounced, undermining of the foundations of society. Tested and tried experience in these terrains of struggle against enemy infiltration of our ranks suggests we use this knowledge to clarify all doubts and uncertainties remaining in relation to these inversions. Proof in hand – photographs, statements from participants in the promiscuous assemblies – those suspected of pro-Hedilla conspiratorial involvement will spontaneously confess all they have to confess – without recourse to the unerring torture reserved for the red hordes.

# TAA

The truth about the missing story concerning the slave market in the Medina of Marrakesh

To alleviate the absence of humour afflicting our collective alignment of stories, I'm going to tell you the tale our colleague from Coketown sidestepped this morning with the excuse that it had disappeared along with the suitcase stolen from the platform in the Bab Dukkala bus station. In fact, there was no such theft and, profiting from his opportune absence from this agreeable garden of readers, I rifled through the bundle of letters, exercise books and notes heaped in his room with a brazenness I should be ashamed of and came across the diary of his journey and now you must forgive me my petty, demeaning behaviour as I read out its contents without adding or deleting a single jot or comma.

However much my parents, may they rest in peace, had already inculcated in me from childhood a visceral antipathy towards Moors and forewarned me of their wheedling trickery, my visit to Marrakesh, in the footsteps of Eusebio, vindicated – and how! – the profound truth behind their feelings and assertions.

I had previously consulted the eyewitness accounts of a few European travellers against the insidious wiles, ways and witchcraft lurking in wait for foreigners, and it occurred

to me that Eusebio might have been the victim of the evil
eye or of spells so characteristic of this superstitious,
backward country. I skimmed several Anglo-Saxon novels
on the topic, as well as half a dozen narratives by cultured,
Frenchified natives, expert in their handling of the language
of Molière.

On my arrival in the ancient Almohad capital, I sought
out a comfortable hotel in the famous square described by
Canetti. On my first recce through the area, I was met by a
well-dressed, welcoming youth who offered in decent
French to accompany me for free to places and monuments
of interest.

Although strengthened by my suspicious nature and
reading material, I was wary and politely refused the offer,
the Moor assured me gently and unassumingly that he was
no '*faux guide*' and wasn't intending artfully to lead me to a
bazaar owned by friends with a view to collecting a
commission on any putative purchase of rugs and craftware.
'I'm a sociology student,' he told me, 'and just want to
practise my languages with foreign visitors.' His well-
mannered behaviour and sensitive words finally convinced
me. Without mentioning Eusebio or the reason for my stay
in Morocco, I explained my desire to broaden my
knowledge in the field of black magic, potions and trance-
inducing ceremonies, as well as the use of talismans and
exorcisms to nullify them. He listened attentively and
declared he could put me in touch with an old woman
renowned for her witchcraft and an awesome, most powerful
wizard.

'Can he put a devil into someone's body, converting the
victim into someone possessed, displace their voice and
personality?'

'That's just what he's good at.'

'Do you think I could interview him and be present at one of his evil-doing rituals?'

'It'll be quite difficult, but one can only try.'

'If you talk to him and persuade him to let me be a fly-on-the wall, I'll reward you handsomely.'

'I told you I'm not after personal gain. Your trust and friendship are enough. But there are some problems and obstacles which require tact and caution.'

I asked him about the nature of the difficulties we were confronting.

'He's an individual who's not easy to get at, he lives in a secret place, absolutely out of bounds to foreigners.'

I tried to find out whether he was referring to a mosque or a cemetery.

'If only he were in one of those two places! Things would be so much easier.'

'Where does he live then?'

My companion paused for thought before he revealed his secret to me, lowering his voice to a whisper. 'He's in the slave market.'

'The slave market?'

'Please, not so loud. If they hear us, we could be put in jail.'

I obeyed him, and we sat down on the half-deserted terrace of a café. 'I thought the French had abolished slavery.'

'That's the official line, but it's not true. Traffic goes on undercover.'

The news shocked me. A clandestine slave market! My interest in tracing Eusebio immediately faded. Breaking this juicy number would be a real scoop! 'Any way we can slip inside?'

My companion fell into a solemn, measured silence. 'I can't answer you now,' he said finally. 'I must first consult

a friend who lives in an adjacent building. If you want I'll
go and see him and we'll meet up in this café late this
afternoon.'

The wait seemed endless. The folkloric attractions of
the square so celebrated by Canetti and other dumbos of
that ilk bored and disappointed me. I rejected out of
hand a snake-charmer's attempt to lace one of his creatures
round my neck and furiously resisted a black dancer,
wearing a red fez, who danced a few steps and shook some
kind of rattlesnake in front of me, in an insistent pursuit
of coins to reward his pathetic, grotesque performance. I
fled the spot and sought refuge in the French restaurant
in the hotel, while I waited for my appointment with the
student.

He appeared after the sonorous call to bring the
Mohammedans to prayer, wearing an inscrutable expression.
'Well, the negotiations were tough, but things can be
resolved if no one notices our presence and we spend the
night on a small terrace, hidden in a bamboo lean-to.'

'That's fine by me.'

He went silent, as if ruminating silently on my reply. 'It's
a very dangerous business for him and for us. To start with,
my friend just didn't want to know, but patience and
promises of help managed to bring him round.'

'Did he ask you for money?'

'Yes, his palm needs greasing.'

'How much does he want?'

'Look, we argued for a long time and never agreed a
figure. But I think forty thousand ryals will do and he'll
take the risk.'

'Forty thousand ryals?'

'Excuse our primitive counting system. It amounts to two
thousand dirhams.'

Mentally I worked out the exchange to pesetas. I'd earn at least twenty times that amount with the scoop.

'Great. Tell him I agree.'

'I must tell him at dinner-time. At midnight, when the streets are almost empty, he'll take us to the lean-to on his terrace. It's right over the slave market.'

'Can I bring my camera?'

The student gave a start. No doubt, mine seemed a bold request.

'I really don't know. I didn't broach the issue with my friend.'

'Tell him it's a little Japanese effort and no flash. I could take photos between the cracks in the bamboo.'

'I can't really give you an answer. I'll have to have a word with him.'

'Go on then. Tell him I'll double my offer.'

'As you like. But I doubt he'll accept.'

'Insist. If the amount I mentioned doesn't make him swallow his fear, I'm prepared to up it.'

He said goodbye looking very anxious and I carried on waiting in the café, now full of regulars playing cards or hypnotised by the shouting and squabbling from the television soap. An hour later he turned up with a coarse-looking fellow dressed Moorish-fashion. He introduced us and translated his friend's conditions into French.

'He says he's really afraid the neighbours will see us and he'll have to find an excuse to move them right away from his house when we go up with him to the lean-to.'

'But will he let me bring a camera?'

They both locked into their incomprehensible jabber and, after a fierce, irritated exchange, the student said he would.

'The poor chap's got a screw loose and is trying to think of a way of getting his neighbours out of the way, a

policeman's family will invite them to the circumcision of
a young relative of his wife. He also wants an advance
payment right now.'

'How much?'

'Half the four thousand you promised. You'll give him
the other half after taking the photos of the slave market.
He also insists you wear a djellaba so nobody will notice
you.'

We shook on the deal, I handed over the two thousand
dirhams to the owner of the lean-to and we agreed to
meet him two hours later. My companion seemed relieved
by the way it had gone and kept telling me to take care.
In the area of the clandestine slave market were lots of spies
and stool-pigeons: en route we remained silent – 'If they
hear you speak French we're done for,' he said – and I had
to wear my hood over my head. Suddenly he seemed to be
distracted and he exclaimed: 'My djellaba! I've got to get
my djellaba right away!' He got up abruptly and said he'd
be back in a few minutes. I waited for a few minutes and
then a few hours, until they shut the café and threw me
into the street. The student had vanished with his djellaba
and my cash.

Back in my hotel room anger and exasperation at the
deceptive, devious behaviour of the Moors made for a
sleepless night and, in the morning, I went to the police
station in the square and gave a detailed account to the duty
officer of the trap they'd set and the wily theft performed.
The reply from the uniformed individual left me cold: 'If
you've swallowed that rubbish and think there's a slave
market in our country you deserve what you got. Your
brand of dupe and fool we call a soft touch and you crop
up as a sorry mess in the jokes and storytelling in the
square.'

That same day I checked out of my hotel and took the

plane to Madrid after an endless stop-over in Casablanca.
I felt full of hatred for that country of thieves and liars. I
thought of the sensible advice from my father, wounded
in the war against Abdelkrim, and of the saying he used to
repeat: 'The only good Moor is a dead'un.'

# ZAA

Extracts from Eusebio★★★'s interrogation in the cells of the Military Special Branch in Sevilla on 25th May 1937 by Colonel★★★, the rapporteur for the case

Judge: Appearing before me as a witness you have sworn to tell the truth, the whole truth and nothing but the truth. First of all repeat your true name.

Witness: Eusebio★★★

Judge: The documentation obtained for you in Granada is clearly fake.

Witness: That's right.

Judge: Out of respect for your brother-in-law and his noble, heroic role in Spain's Movement of Salvation we will put this issue to one side on condition you cooperate with us and answer my questions frankly and honestly.

Witness: Yes, milord.

Judge: In what circumstances did you meet Veremundo and Basilio?

Witness: Thanks to my brother-in-law's intervention I was taken from death row in Melilla and transferred to the peninsula, to the Military Rehabilitation Centre in Granada, in effect to the section headed by Doctor V. M. For several weeks I was isolated and received electric shock treatment, and was only allowed to speak to the nurses and the military chaplain. When I began my recovery and threw off ideas and habits contracted in the Republican period, Comrade

Basilio visited me and offered to help me in the re-education process.

Judge: And what was the nature of this help?

Witness: He indoctrinated me in the spiritual values of the Crusade, the Fatherland for which José Antonio and the other Martyrs had fought and spilt their blood.

Judge: Which names and figures did he set you as examples?

Witness: José Antonio, Ramiro Ledesma, Onésimo Redondo . . . Well, the men sacrificed for God and for Spain.

Judge: What about Franco? Did he make any mention of Franco?

Witness: Sometimes, but less often.

Judge: Didn't a clever person like yourself note any reticence in relation towards him and Queipo? By the bye, what did he say about the Carlists?

Witness: He used to tell jokes about them.

Judge: About Franco as well?

Witness: No, not about Franco.

Judge: Are you sure about that?

Witness: Perhaps he did, I just don't remember.

Judge: I'll give you a couple of hours to ponder. The guard will escort you to the guard room. You can ask him for water or coffee if you want some but he won't let you sleep.

( . . .)
( . . .)

Judge: Did you use the break to reflect?

Witness: Yes, milord.

Judge: You know as well as I do Basilio and Veremundo's

sexual proclivities, the nature of the relations they maintained with the youths in their squads, am I not right?

Witness: Yes, milord.

Judge: Did he broach the subject with you?

Witness: In his educational talks he criticised my vulgar, base tastes, severely reprehended my roughing it with Mustafas and hairy labourers. He exalted noble love for blond, smooth-cheeked adolescents, after the manner of the great artists and philosophers of antiquity.

Judge: Did he ever embark on any relationship of this type with you?

Witness: No, milord.

Judge: Did he invite you to go to his 'initiation into manhood' parties?

Witness: Our relationship was purely patient–doctor. He sustained and glorified his ideals against my lack of dignity and valour. I felt so bad, so sick, so corrosively sad that I accepted internment as a just and moral imprisonment, an indispensable cathartic experience.

Judge: All these reports and information are on your friend Basilio's file; contrary to what he'd agreed with you, he kept them in a secret place to use them in case of necessity. You should know his devotion to your person concealed interests of another kind, a double game you have helped us elucidate.

Witness: I swear I don't know what you're talking about.

Judge: Basilio and Veremundo recruited accomplices from the ranks of Falangist discontents and even from amongst individuals like yourself, with dubious pasts, in order to oppose the leadership of the Caudillo, sanctioned by the decree of Unification. With a curriculum as black as yours they could make you their plaything, manipulate you at will. You were an ideal pawn in their subversive plans and in conniving with enemy undercover agents. That's what convinces us that playing the card of your file, your Marxist sympathies and sexual inversion, they told you about the plans they were hatching for a future Republican state and their strategies for taking power.

Witness: No, neither he nor Veremundo talked politics with me. They incited me to go after Greek love all right. To be a virile, active lover.

Judge: See how you're beginning to remember things and tell the truth? Just carry on pulling the thread and let the ball unravel. You've only got a few hours. The guard will take you to your cell so you can reflect in comfort. Your statement is of central importance in the case we're mounting against your colleagues' betrayal of the Cause. Think of your own self-interest. Don't ever forget we have all we need to crush you like an insect if you don't heed us. A clear denunciation of the activities of that stinking band of pederasts and enemy agents can save you from the destiny that awaited you in Melilla. We hold no brief to review your legal position or abrogate the agreement with your brother-in-law: on the contrary, if the patriotic, nationalist fervour in Sevilla is stifling you, we can get you a safe pass to Portugal or Tangiers. On condition, of course, that you deliver a definitive statement on Veremundo and Basilio's manoeuvring.

( . . .)
( . . .)

Judge: Have you given the matter careful thought?
Witness: Yes.
Judge: Are you ready to sign the declaration we've written for you?
Witness: Yes.

Judge: Here it is. Read it aloud from the second paragraph.

Witness: 'The signatory affirms of his own free will, without duress, that he took part in a clandestine meeting held on 21st April.'

(brief interruption) Milord, I was in Sevilla, not Granada, around that time.

Judge: Forget that bilge! You were in Granada as it says in the statement! Get on with it!

Witness: 'A meeting during which Comrade Basilio described Franco as a "scoundrel" and "traitor", and urged contacts be established with cadres and members of the Falange and the National Syndicalist Youth opposed to the decree of unification, to join forces with discontented officers and chiefs and despatch clandestine emissaries to red territory. Comrade Veremundo expressed his total support for these plans and demanded those present swore an oath of secrecy and to sacrifice their lives to keep the ideals of the Crusade free of opportunists and carpet-baggers, the conspiratorial assembly lasted some six hours and was attended by fifty-odd people, amongst whom the declaree recognised, apart from Veremundo and Basilio, their aides and thirty youths from their squad. Similarly he noted the presence of a stranger who, he deduced, was the group's contact with Republican intelligence services. The witness equally states he received no further instructions nor was he summoned to other meetings at more advanced stages of the conspiracy.'

Judge: Is the statement endorsed by the addition 'read and approved'?

Witness: Yes, milord.

Judge: Right and now lips sealed! Not a word about appearing in this trial! Go home and you'll be brought the right instructions. If you keep collaborating with us, we'll keep to everything I told you. We won't interfere in your private life, but you must remain totally loyal and faithful to us.

Note by the clerk: 'The witness was at all times fully conscious, competent to understand and express himself. No fluctuations of memory were detected, and his language was at every juncture, fluent, coherent and correct in manner.'

# AYN

## The Stork-Men

I'm a woman into magical realism, an avid reader of García
Márquez, the Allende gal and their high-flying disciples.
I'm just wild about novels and stories seething with colourful
characters and awesome incident: sage grannies, clouds
raining blood, children on the wing, galleons mysteriously
beached in lush virgin jungle. These *romans de pays chauds*,
as a defender of anaemic, worn-out literary notions dubbed
them, bring a new sap and vitality, a pinch of poetry into
the prosaic confines of our lives. Consequently, when I
heard my esteemed co-reader in the Circle tell the story
of *The Thousand Nights Less One*, which referred to the
storks' nest near Eusebio's little place in the Casbah, next to
the *mechouar*, I recalled my compatriot Ali Bey's paragraphs
on these long-shanked migrators whose company he
enjoyed in Marrakesh thanks to a gullible sultan.

According to an old Moroccan tradition, Berber peasants
think of storks as human beings who, in order to travel
and see the world, temporarily adopt their birdly shape and
resume their original form on returning home. Thus, when
I reached Marrakesh in pursuit of the elusive Eusebio, I
decided to renounce my risky, fruitless investigations and,
thanks to the gracious help of historian Hamid Triki, I
headed towards the ancient hospice for storks adjacent to
the mosque of Ben Yussef.

After much enquiring and promenading I came across Dar Belarx and its keeper. Encouraged by my generous tip, he produced a bunch of keys and led me through a side door, along a gloomy porch, to a huge and magnificent yet filthy and abandoned courtyard. All manner of rubble and rubbish covered the central space, blessed with a fountain, beautiful arcades, mouldings in side rooms, friezes of tiles firmly resisting the passage of time. There were infinite messes of pigeon feathers and droppings, even a fresh corpse of a member of the species, attracted like its confrères, by the benign silence of the place. The hospice had been closed a century earlier, upon the death of one of its founder's grandsons.

I mentioned the myth of the stork-men to my companion. To my great surprise, he corrected my characterisation. It was no myth, it was the unsullied truth. He himself had a neighbour who migrated to Europe and returned home a few months later, after recovering his normal shape. He lived right up that alley and, without more ado, I was introduced to him.

The metamorphoser – what better nomer? – was a calm, peaceful old man, similar in looks to those attributed by colleagues to Eusebio, with intense blue eyes and an immaculate white beard, seated in the doorway to his house, his right hand perched on the top of his walking-stick. To avoid vexatious preambles, I'll give you his story straight, be it genuine or not, fruit of an invention of his own harvesting, or borrowed from folklore.

'Forty odd years ago, my wife – may God preserve her in her glory – got a permit to work in a French textile factory and emigrated in order to increase our modest income, leaving me in charge of the children. To begin with, she sent news like clockwork together with a transfer representing her monthly savings; but gradually the money turned to a trickle, without any comforting missive. Such a strange, lengthy silence, raising apprehension and troubling questions, plunged me into deep melancholy. My letters went unanswered; my request for telephonic communication likewise. I asked after her via a neighbour, also contracted by a textile firm in the same region. Her laconic telegram – "well and working" – not only was not soothing, it stoked my unease. If she was well, why so silent? Had she forgotten she was a wife and mother of four? At night, I tossed and turned restlessly in bed. In the meantime, the possibilities of getting a passport had shrunk: the crisis and unemployment in Christian lands closed doors on foreigners and the French Consulate would not grant a visa to an artisan like myself: a humble cobbler. They demanded bank statements and goodness knows what else. In a word: I had to give up. But I dreamt and dreamt ever more vividly of making the journey. And one day, while gazing at the storks nesting on the battlements of the royal palace, I said in my heart of hearts, if only I was like them and could fly to where my wife's working, to the distant sweatshop in Epinal. As if fired by a premonition, I went to see my eldest brother: I told him I'd decided to go to Europe and handed my children over to him for their temporary care and education. That fretful phase of my life was abruptly at an end.

'The following day, I was aloft with a flock of storks in an ineffable state of bliss and delight. The world was at once miniature and immense: toy towns and landscapes, seas gleaming like mirrors, white mountains . . . My altitude, lightness and speed of movement granted me a feeling of superiority over humans, slow as turtles, tiny like insects. Intoxicated by our gliding in precise, purposeful formation, I flew joyfully towards the prosperous, enlightened

continent whence the Christians had come apparently to
educate us and offer us work while they were about it.
They were weeks of freedom and pleasure, beyond frontiers
and the stamping of travel documents. Without any papers
we crossed compartmentalised territories, transgressed their
mean-spirited laws, avoided customs and police controls,
mocked the miserly discrimination of visas. Once over a
great chain of mountains, snow-covered like the Atlas, the
panorama changed: the fields were greener, the woods
denser and more frequent, ochre-tiled villages gave way to
grey-slate roofs. We followed a river valley, its sides lined
with factories and cities. A few days later, after long days
of flight and nightly stops on towers and belfries, I felt my
energy waning, went out of rhythm with my companions,
fell irrevocably behind, flapped my wings with difficulty.
Unable even to hover, I plummeted and landed in a garden
as best I could.

'My appearance surprised the owner of the house, a
Frenchman in his forties, who was pruning shrubs and
tidying up the lawn with his shears. "Look, darling Aysha,
it's a stork," he shouted. My beloved wife's name made my
heart miss a beat. Who was that fellow and how dare he be
so familiar? When she peeped out of the backdoor I almost
fainted. I stared at her till my eyes were awash with tears.
"How incredible," she said in Frankish tongue, "there are
lots of them in my country. I'm sure that where she's from."
She walked over, didn't recognise me, gently caressed my
plumage. "How tame! She must have fallen ill and can't fly
anymore. I'll look after her and feed her on raw fish. In
our country they say it brings luck: a guest sent from heaven,
whom we must respect and offer hospitality."

'Aysha's tender, welcoming words deepened, did not
soften my grief. Her use of "we" and friendly attitude
towards the individual confirmed my suspicions: she was his

concubine, shared his bed and table. Bewildered and bitter,
I wondered whether they had children. I was afraid I'd hear
a baby's cry and inspected the washing basket and
fortunately saw neither nappies nor infant clothing. But the
previous feeling of superiority and pride that had possessed
me in the ether transmuted into impotent rage. Two steps
away from my wife and her lover, with my clumsy shanks
and grating croaks, I was unable to react against her adultery.
Aysha's maternally tender affections, the zeal with which
she cared for me, chose my food, built a kind of nest on
the roof of the garden shed, undermined, rather than
enhanced, my temporary birdly state. My appearance
reminded her of her country, she showered me with
caresses and treats, but at dusk, when they both returned
from work – she from her sweatshop, he from the branch
of a big bank – they shut themselves in their house and left
me one-legged on my nest.

'After the first melancholy weeks, my spirits began to
rise: I decided to take the offensive. I abandoned my nest
of misfortune and without a by-your-leave slipped into the
house. At first, the intruder tried to chase me out, but she
stopped him.

' "This stork's a blessed creature who reminds me of all I
left behind. If she wants to live inside, she will. God sent
her to us and her wishes will be met."

'The guy oozed bad-temper: "This is all very poetic, but
who'll clean the shit up?"

' "I will! Haven't I told you a thousand times it's a sacred
animal?"

'Although he snorted something scornful about India and
her cows, she shrugged her shoulders and imposed her
will: henceforth, if I felt like it, I'd live with them night and
day.

'The new situation created by my wife's energy and

determination favoured my plans for revenge. I took advantage of both their absences during work hours and sniffed around the furniture and nooks and crannies of the house: I could see for myself how Aysha kept photos of her children like gold bars, put her entire wages in a savings account, and regularly sent home part by postal order. The intruder paid for everything, the shopping, my fish and leeches, the gas and electricity bills. Such signs of provision for our future, added to the attention she paid me, strengthened my resolve: I did more of the business on the guy's personal items and clothes, made myself comfortable in his bed.

'As I dallied there, the domestic rows and squabbles got worse.

' "You're not going to let her dirty the sheets?"

' "If she soils the sheets, I'll wash them. The poor girly" (she always referred to me in the feminine) "after such a long journey and then falling ill, feels at home here, is part of the family."

'I pretended to yield to the intruder's irritation, nobly left the terrain, waited till they put out the light and he began to stir and stroke her before I swooped on the bed and soiled it. Immediately he switched on the bed-side light.'

' "That's enough playing around! I'll deal with her now! Enough is enough!"

' "You so much as touch one feather and you'll be sorry! You just listen to me: I'm sick up to here of your disgusting fiddling. Let me sleep in peace!"

' "If you want to sleep, sleep; but not with her. I've told you a thousand times I can't stand the bird!"

' "Well, If you can't stand her, clear off to the sofa! Personally, I don't intend to separate from her!"

' "Anyone would think she was your husband! Ever since she came, you've been behaving like a loony. These manias

and witches' tales come from your country, not from any
modern, civilised nation!"

' "Hey, my country is better than yours. This stork's mine
and, if you don't like her, I'm off and Happy Christmas."

'From that night on there were daily quarrels. I wanted
to sleep in my bed, next to my wife, and the intruder finally
conceded and migrated to the sofa. I felt Aysha preferred
me and was thinking about me. Sometimes she sat at the
kitchen table and wrote letters home, to the address next to
the hospice for storks founded centuries ago. She cohabited
with the Gentile like a dog with a cat. When she went out
I flew to the shed awning and perched on the nest. I was
afraid the intruder would slice my head off with a knife or
club me to death. I was comforted by my victory and
began to recover a taste for flight. One day, after devouring
my ration of fish, I bid a silent farewell to Aysha, looked
out for my flock overhead, flew up and headed back to
Marrakesh.

'I recovered my human form as soon as I arrived. I turned
up at home as if I'd just left and hugged my children. My
brother had diligently looked after them, they'd been to
school and, when they saw me, they danced with joy.
Underneath the clock in my bedroom was a pile of letters
from Aysha. They spoke of the stork's visit, of how she
missed her country. She was still working in the textile
factory to meet her savings target and to be able to buy a
shop on her return. When she came back two years later,
she beamed radiantly and arrived loaded with presents. I
forgave her, of course, I forgave her: I forgot her infidelity
and lived happily with her till God wanted her at His
side and she was buried in Bab Dukkala.

'I never told her or anybody else of the truth about my
visit, except for my neighbour and a gentleman of
European origins whose friend from the Rif died in a traffic

accident and who had lived ever since away from the world, writing verse and seeking solace every afternoon in the mosque of Ben Yussef. His name was Eusebio.

'I remember he listened very carefully and then wrote down word for word the very same story I've just told you.'

# GHAYN

A Viscontian spotlight on the end of Veremundo and
Basilio

Like many young people of my generation, my upbringing
has been cinematic rather than literary. I prefer to see the
pages of my favourite novels translated into images,
witnessing high-tension dramas, contemplating the whole
range of emotions of the human soul on the protagonists'
faces. That's why I'm bored to tears by works which adapt
with difficulty to the screen, Joyce, Céline, Thomas
Bernhard and others of that kind, like Count Julian about
whom so many mind-numbing theses have been compiled.

My colleague's tale of the political trial rigged in April
1937 against Eusebio's Falange leader friends, a trial made
possible by the sexual practices of the accused and their rites
of 'initiation into manhood' brought back adolescent
memories of an old Visconti film about similar happenings
in the same decade with the Nazi leaders of the SA.

Wanting to reconstruct the facts, referred to tangentially
in the MSB report, and the statement extracted under
duress from the unfortunate poet, object of this investigation,
I consulted the documents accessible to the general public
in the provincial archive of Granada, as well as those
transferred to Madrid in the postwar period yet never came
across the military file dealing with the summary judgement;
that was probably destroyed by the investigation agency

itself in order to erase all trace of the somewhat unedifying case. The only things I got from my interviews with half a dozen Old Blue Shirts were three photos of the accused and an original letter from Basilio to an anonymous acting lieutenant. One of the ex-youths of the phalanx gave the exact date of the events, 11th May 1937, and some of the circumstances of how his leaders were trapped in that mortal ambush.

Had they conspired against the decree inspired by Franco to unify the Falange, National Syndicalist Youth and the Movement's monarchists and traditionalists? They probably had, I was told. Basilio and Veremundo were hardline Falangists: they considered such a fusion a monstrous mish-mash, contrary to José Antonio's ideals and aspirations. For several weeks they'd been in the sights of the MSB who were on the lookout for an opportunity to catch them hands on bums. One of the adolescents in the group, a Special Branch plant, told them the day and time of the initiation ceremonies. A strong contingent of security forces surrounded the school building in the early hours and burst into the leaders' private rooms with a round of machine-gun fire.

An Old Blue Shirt I chatted to has a portrait of the founder of the Falange, with this handwritten scrawl by Basilio: *José Antonio, silent, stately professor of absence.* He also handed me four manuscript lines by the poet from Tangiers, whose name he did not recall, dedicated to Veremundo:

> *God drives upwards!*
> *Excelsior! Excelsior!*
> *Way above the clouds!*
> *To the moon! To the stars!*

Another one quoted me lines by the Martyr, learned by heart from Basilio's lips:

*It was a victory hymn clouds and waves*
*at a proud, majestic pace*
*sang to Spanish ships*
*envoys of the Iberian Race!*

I put my hands on several type-written sheets of quotes and phrases that served as a starting point for glosses and doctrinal commentary:

*Blue shirt, categorical, emblematic sign:*
*Affirming, aggressive uniform, sublimely totalitarian*
*Yoke and Arrows, incarnation of*
*youthful pride, of brave, bold energies,*
*able to revive the Hispanic fatherland,*
*crucible of faith and spiritualism.*

The photo of a hatless Basilio, in Falangist boots and kit, his hair unkempt, shows a well-built, blond youth puffing his chest out and displaying a smiling set of even, white teeth. He looks about thirty – born 1903 according to the Baza parish records – and exudes a confidence in the future which the sound and fury of those years very quickly gave the lie to.

Veremundo's is a simple, blurry identity card. They also let me see a snapshot of him, squeezed between the lads from his cohort, like a trainer with his football team.

This is the only material evidence I collected. The scraps of information about the attack on the Falange Training School are vague, riddled with contradictions and flagrant anachronisms. Did they attempt to resist and exchange fire, as one interviewee claimed? Did Veremundo die Star in hand, as another Old Blue Shirt reckons?

Were they shot to smithereens where they staged their orgies?

Faced with the need to write this story or chapter agreed for these peaceful weeks in the garden, I was suddenly rescued by Visconti's film to which I referred.

('Literature is the quickest, easiest means of diffusion for the corruptors of our age-old purity. The new Spain's mission is to burn and destroy whatever is poisoning it. The spectacle of Masonic, Communist and Jewish books on the bonfire is highly educational and cathartic.'

I quote from memory these lines written by an intellectual fellow-traveller of the Movement, which danced round my head to the stirring musical accompaniment of *The Twilight of the Gods*.)

Let's sketch in the scene: Basilio has just toasted the ideals of José Antonio and his heroic Blue Shirts. – five arrows of light! – who fell in the Crusade. He shares his glass with one of the youths and soon lips and breath are harmonised. Naked from the waist up, they feel and touch each other's naked torsoes. Veremundo's gramophone bellows out a beery 'Cara al sol' and 'ich hatt' eine kamaraden'. In the half-dark I can make out fair-haired youths, smooth-chested and beardless, but wearing Falange berets. One of them pours out the wine and keeps the glasses filled. I listen to Basilio's speechifying on the synthesis of epic and lyric, on virile ardour and purity modelled on Greek and Teutonic ideals: 'Nobly erect like ears of wheat, ready to sacrifice your lives to defeat the plebeian dregs of a soulless, prostituted Spain.' When he snuffs out the candles, the scant light is gone. Now I catch glimpses of promiscuous members, body around body on bunks and mattresses. The gramophone huskily blares the bellicose voices which exalt death, completely oblivious to her imminent arrival. 'That's a corker, and a fine pair of balls,' says Basilio. 'None of that pansy poofery for me, we're valiant, upstanding men.' The tune and words *I had a comrade/the best of the lot/we marched together/ we advanced together/to the beat of the drum* cloak embraces, couplings, alcoholic harangues. It's 2 a.m., the implacable hour of the reaper.

Don't ask me about the butchery. I don't know how it happened and Visconti cut it to a brief sequence. Did the supposed ring-leaders of the conspiracy die there and then or were they executed soon after, and with or without trial? Nobody could give me a straight answer. In the scenario of sodomite Saturnalia wine mingled with blood. Eusebio's letter dated in Sevilla read by our fellow reader in the first week in this peaceful, make-believe garden probably figures among the documents saved from the attack.

# THIRD WEEK

# FAA

## A truncated tale and a turn-up for the books

An Arabist by training, forged in university lecture rooms under the guidance of prestigious masters, my obsidian approach to the schema or matrix for the quest for Eusebio will per force introduce a touch of scientific rigour unfortunately lacking in previous orientalist or would-be Moorish contributions from my fellow readers in the Circle, not to mention the barefaced plagiarism by one of their number of a story by a Spanish writer published in *Le Monde Diplomatique* a few years ago . . .

*Voices: who, who?*
*The unflinching narrator:*

I'll also ignore the blatant anachronism of some of my friends who slot into 1936 the use of electrical shocks for medical purposes when the fact is this strange, dubious therapy arrived in Spain only in the following decade. Don't ply me now with the pleasure of unlikely imaginings or other tall stories! History is history, and a novelist must submit thereto!

*Disapproving murmurs disturbed the tranquil arbour, followed by throat-clearing, coughs and well wells. The co-reader waited impassively for peace to reign once more.*

Thanks to those distinguished professors – translators to
boot of the illustrious seer from the Euphrates whose work
would seem to be the inspiration of the most progressive
bards in the West if chronology didn't persist in upholding
the contrary – I immersed myself in the sources of the
cultures of Damascus and Baghdad, cradle of the refined
Andalusian civilisation of the Caliphate – a true 'garden of
poets', nostalgically serenaded even now by contemporary
troubadours – a civilisation violently destroyed by hordes of
Moorish and Berber Almoravides and Almohades. For this
reason – the devastation wrought by the 'swarms of African
locusts', to use the expression coined by a famous historian
– I don't share literary Moorophilia or the more base philias
of some colleagues in the trade and tell it for what it is:
mere folklore. The Maghreb's peripheral nature in relation
to the flourishing centres of Arab culture explains why my
first dip into the waters has been so recent and fortuitous:
impelled, as you know, by the Eusebio enigma.

'On my arrival to Mur-rākuš, after an interminable stop-
over in Casablanca airport, I parked my suitcase in a hotel
and headed, like one more tourist, to the renowned square
of *Ŷāmi'al-finā*.[1] Night had just fallen and at the little gas-
lit foodstalls customers consumed *bayṣara*[2] and other
succulent winter dishes. Despite the cold, numerous *mur-
rākušiy-yīn* were crowded round the *al-ḥalaqa*,[3] where an
aged *halāiqī*[4] was reciting stories of *Ŷuḥa*[5] imported from

---

[1] Literally 'mosque in the courtyard or square'. According to the most
popular version, 'gathering for executions', a name derived from a legend
according to which rioters against the sultan were hung in the present space
of the square.
[2] A bean soup very popular in Morocco.
[3] A circle formed by people round a performance.
[4] The actor, musician or narrator of *ḥalaqa*.
[5] A famous young character in the Arab world, known for his witty, clever
and comic ways.

the *Mašriq*.[6] In the next ring of spectators, a rhapsodist was humming a bitter-sweet melody in *al-'amāzīgiyi-ya*.[7] After wandering a few minutes to avoid the begging *tarbūš*[8] of the *al-gī-niy-yūn*[9] and the camera-prompting tinkle of the *as-saqqāīn*,[10] there called *al-gar-rābīn*, I came across a *al-ḥalaqa* whose theatre interested me because I'd read the thesis devoted to it by a colleague who graduated with me, a Moorophile and ethnologist into other odds and sods: a door-stopper of some three hundred pages on the *al-ḥaḍra*[11] of the troubadours of Abi Rah-hāl.[12]

'The secularised followers of Sayyidī Raḥ-ḥal al-Budālī[13] whose initiatory *silsila*[14] go back, according to legend, to Al-Yāzūlī and to Ăs-šadilī,[15] are famous in Morocco for the *at-taḥay-yur*,[16] during which, in a state of trance, they abandon themselves to ecstatic dances around a stove on which the *muqrāy̆*[17] is hotting up. The *muqad-dam*,[18] whom I greeted in classical Arabic, ceremoniously offered me a stool so I could watch the *ḥaḍra* in comfort.

'The *ar-raḥ-ḥa'lī*[19] *al-matbu'*, dressed in simple breeches,

---

[6] The Middle East.
[7] Berber dialect from the central Atlas Mountains.
[8] A kind of fez very popular in Morocco.
[9] A brotherhood of dancers and musicians, descendants of slaves originally from southern Saharan Africa. Their name is a distortion of Guinea.
[10] Water-sellers dressed in traditional clothes, wearing broad-brimmed hats who distribute water kept in their skin-bags (*al gerba*) and shake their bells to attract customers or get money for a photo from tourists.
[11] An assembly during which the devotees of *Sayyidī Raḥ-ḥal* recite their litanies and execute their ecstatic dances.
[12] See the next note.
[13] A mystic who founded the *raḥ-ḥāliya* (died in 1543). Said to have had great charismatic presence.
[14] Literally chain: spiritual genealogy.
[15] Two Sufi masters whose teaching spread to a great part of the Arab world.
[16] The frenetic dance of the *raḥ-ḥāliyin*.
[17] A metal kettle, heated by the stove till the water boils and evaporates.
[18] An administrative helper. In this case, responsible for the trance session.
[19] The *raḥ-ḥāli* 'marked', 'sealed', by the *at-teb'a* or stamp of *Sayyidī Raḥ-ḥal*.

barefoot, hirsute, with long locks, was swaying in rhythm
with the *al-bandīr*[20] and the flute, invoking the help of the
Prophet, of *Say-yidī Raḥ-ḥal* and the remaining saints of
the *Tas-sawt*.[21] He leaned his chest towards his knees, his
hands gripping his back, to an increasingly fever-pitched
cadence. A *malā'ikiy-ya*[22] imitated his movements, possessed,
as the *muqad-dam* explained, by the *Lal-la Malīka*.[23] The
*raḥ-ḥali*, now kneeling next to the *muqrāŷ*, gaze askance, hair
dishevelled and soaked in sweat, brought his lips to the *as-
sunbula*[24] that was rising from the spout of the kettle. After
the *at-taslīm*,[25] accompanied by the orisons and litanies of
those present, he rose from the ground, asked the gathering
to repeat his words – *al-baraka! al-baraka!*[26] – and seized the
kettle firmly, poured a stream of scalding water into his
mouth and began to sprinkle the public with his *aš-šakwa*[27]
without giving the least manifestation of pain. It was then,
whilst he contemplated the *ŷadba*[28] of the *mawlǎ al-muqrāŷ*,[29]
the whiteness of the *as-sunbula*, that I imagined Eusebio,
*maskūn*[30] for Mimoun or Hamou the *ŷaz-zār*,[31] in a similar
scene and . . .'

*The jeers from the co-readers gathered in the delightfully cultivated*

---

[20] A big drum used by some brotherhoods in their street ceremonies and
processions.
[21] A river that crosses the region where *Sayyidī Raḥ-ḥal* and *Abi 'Aumar* lie,
next to Mur-rākuš.
[22] A woman possessed.
[23] A famous *ŷinn* or genie of the female sex.
[24] The steam coming from the spout of the *muqrāŷ*.
[25] An act of submission to the saint.
[26] The blessing.
[27] A sprinkling from the mouth with magic, healing powers.
[28] An ecstatic dance favoured by popular brotherhoods.
[29] Literally, the master of the *muqrāŷ*, the one handling the kettle of boiling
water.
[30] A man possessed.
[31] Two *ŷinun* (plural of *ŷin*) frequently invoked in brotherhood rituals.

*garden, to whom he had distributed the text before reading it, with his notes and canonical reproduction of Arabic script, drowned his voice. Taking advantage of the hullabaloo, somebody climbed on to the podium from which the Arabist narrated his story and read Sempronio's warning to his master Calixto in the eighth act of* La Celestina:

'Master, stop being so long-winded, leave off the poetry, for it's not right to use language that isn't common to all, which all don't use, which few understand. Say: "although the sun sets" and everyone will know what you're on about. And have some jam, and you'll keep going a good while yet.'

*Curt applause abruptly ended the session.*

# QAAF

A chance reference to Tangiers in the story told by our colleague in the Readers' Circle had the wit and virtue to inspire me and suddenly open wide the sluicegates of my constrained imagination. Although a lot of water had flowed from the time of the Spanish civil war, when the city still enjoyed its international status, to the days in the mid-sixties when I set foot there and tried to recreate its likeness and immerse myself in the atmosphere reigning thirty-bit years before, thanks to Emilio Sanz de Soto, Tangier's living archive of memories. With his precious help and a handful of black and white photos, I was suddenly plunged into the turbulent world of petty intrigue of the summer of 1937 and from the fishermen's quayside I watched set sail the liner in which Eusebio was travelling.

Casually elegant, a felt hat concealing his incipient baldness, carrying a simple, if rather extravagant leather case, he passed through the formalities of customs, still nestling at the foot of the fortified wall, by the row of royal cannons ready to shoot, one could say, at the hypothetical intruder come to wake them from their mouldering slumbers, their deep, comatose sleep. His documentation was in order and, once he'd done the necessary, he entrusted his case to a native carrier and gave him the address of a pension on the avenida de España.

His first port of call, after a quick shower and cursory tidy up, was to Rafael D., the renowned cardiologist and silver-tongued bard, whose unexpected entry into the ranks of the Falange and murky services to the Movement had upset friends and patients alike: an opportunist change of coat or, as some wags put it, a quick crawl across from the Zoco Chico, from the Republican dialogues of the Café-pension Fuentes to the front-line terrace of the large Café Central.

'You over here? What a surprise! I thought you were on the other side, with the poet friends we used to see together. I still remember the night when we drank coffee together after a recital given by poor Federico.'

'Nobody told you I'd arrived?'

'Are you now, by any chance, Eugenio Asensio?'

'Yes, and here's the letter from provincial headquarters in Sevilla. I was told to contact you.'

(Did it really happen that way? Did they really exchange words in the doctor's surgery or private abode the day he arrived?

'Probably not,' said Emilio. 'The city was rife with rumours and every newcomer was suspect. Although the two sides were clearly defined, many inhabitants of Tangiers drifted from one to another or met in cafés of proven neutrality, with their compatriots from England or central Europe. The Italians lined up behind Mussolini and the anti-Popular Front French.')

The poet who introduced himself to the Café Fuentes circle had managed to escape, almost miraculously, he said, from the territory under rebel control. His Republican sympathies, friendship with Altolaguirre and Emilio Prados, his non-conformist poems published in various avant-garde magazines were enough to convert him into the ideal prey for the pack of Fascist playboys and Falangist thugs. Thanks

to bribes and inside help he managed to take refuge in
Portugal and reach Tangiers from there with forged papers.
His passport identified him as one Eugenio Asensio, born
in the Canaries, a small businessman.

One of those present had known him in Cádiz, when he
was still Eusebio, and confirmed what he'd said and done.
The Fash, he warned, used to gather on the opposite
pavement and then meet their Italian co-religionaries in the
Café Roma, near the Hotel Minzah. They'd established
the Spanish Falange headquarters in a small villa on the
calle Dante and were attempting to set up a consular office
to rival the official delegation representing the Republican
government. They had files on everybody who gathered in
the Café Fuentes and dispatched reports on them to
military command in Tetuan.

He soon won the fraternity's trust. Though reserved by
nature and not fond of speechifying, he appalled everyone
with his sober but detailed account of the executions and
massacres carried out by the insurgents in Sevilla and Granada.
The position of Spanish Republicans in Tangiers was
precarious, the city was swarming with spies in the pay of
the Fascists and Nazis, there were rumours of preventive
actions against red ring-leaders with the backing or a
blessed blind-eye from the international administration.

(The kidnapping of a Communist plumber, planned in
the headquarters on calle Dante, and his subsequent dispatch
to Ceuta, handcuffed, a chloroform-soaked handkerchief
stuffed in his mouth, in the boot of Rafael D.'s car, had
ended disastrously. Those awaiting the captive Bolshevik
could only take charge of his corpse. Their prey had
suffocated to death.

Had this incident occurred before or after Eusebio's arrival
and his secret contacts with the renowned cardiologist?)

Apparently they met up in a bathhouse, tucked away in

the labyrinth of alleys in the Medina, where they coupled with their respective lovers. After preliminary massages and joyful promiscuity with catamites in a quiet tenebrarium, they drank tea alone in a tea-room where the boozy-eyed French owner served them personally, dressed in exotic Rif mountain garb. There, Rafael D. passed on instructions from local headquarters and Eusebio told of interesting information gleaned from his chats with the regulars in the Café Fuentes.

He underwent a strange change in appearance. The slender, delicate poet, admirer of Cernuda and friend of Emilio Prados, began to go fat and flabby. His cheeks puffed out, his forehead filled with ridges and cracks. His shirts and trousers struggled to contain his swollen neck and pappy flesh and he had to change his wardrobe, buy a completely new stock. It was attributed by his acquaintances to the climate and over-eating: too much couscous, paella, roast leg of lamb, tapas and table wines, honey cakes, jams, syrups. After two years in Tangiers he was almost unrecognisable. He was often to be seen in cake shops, downing croissants, cream tarts and chocolate cake. His insatiable appetite, abuse of liqueurs and dessert wines coincided exactly with his personality's shocking transformation on the day of Franco's victory: he ceased to be likeable, modest, a man keen on art and literature, and became ambitious, calculating and arrogant. Overnight he broke off all relations with his friends and paraded in patriotic gatherings and with the retinue of the new plenipotentiary minister from Spain. He spoke casually of the city's imminent liberation from its 'cosmopolitan scurvy'. He occupied a front-row seat in the official podium during march pasts by youth organisations and the Royal Palace bodyguard. Eugenio Asensio's obese figure stood out as eccentric and enigmatic among Tangiers' variegated fauna: he had purchased a vast

trading space in the Zoco Grande and took advantage of
the closure of the foreign exchange offices to extend his
array of grocery and drink stores and bazaars via bribes
and fixes. His leasing company took over the empty base of
the British Women's Association and acquired exclusive
rights to represent Bière La Lorraine. A burly goon in cap
and uniform chauffeured him around and he mistreated
the natives, whom he nevertheless welcomed at night into
the boudoir of his luxurious villa on el Monte.

Nobody knew how he had amassed such a fortune or
established friendly links with the Khalifa and High
Commissioner. Someone saw him whip the face of a young
bootblack who'd crouched by his feet, with brush and box,
without asking prior permission. Then at the same speed
with which he built his empire, he squandered his property
and business and faded from sight.

Had he set up in the French Protectorate and collaborated
with the Vichy secret services, as he'd previously served
Franco's? That's what the sharp tongues of Tangiers
reckoned, but no valid proof corroborated such gossip.

'He was the kind who would pay to sell himself,' Emilio
Sanz de Soto told me.

In his library he had a photo of Eusebio with Manolo
Altolaguirre and Concha Méndez: a bright-eyed, sincere-
looking young man, the antipodes of the man he later
showed me, either alone or in company.

'Take a good look,' he concluded after a long pause. 'He
didn't even possess the wit the devil granted Dorian Gray.'

# KAAF

You must take a right turning off the main road from Marrakesh to Beni Mella in the direction of Sidi Rahhal, till you reach the village of Al Attauia, the resting-place of the remains of Buya Ahmad, one of the three patron saints of the sacred territory of Tasaut. Lame-legged carts, ramshackle lorries and all manner of weary, tottering perambulators there await the arrival of pilgrims in order to transport them along a three-kilometre dust-covered track that leads to the sanctuary of Buya Omar. The landscape is the plain of Hauz: fields of wheat, barley and cotton, olive groves, prickly pear hedges, small agricultural settlements.

When I arrived led by the hand of my friend Khadija Maamuni – an expert in the rites of the *zawiya* and very familiar with the terrain – the sun shone at its zenith, enhancing the whiteness and simplicity of the Morabite's shrine. Two smaller hermitages, with the tombs of his daughter and one of his grandsons, also welcomed to their bosom a long row of visitors anxious to gain the grace of an eventual cure. After we'd parked on the outskirts of the village and entrusted the vehicle's care to a friend of hers to avoid vengeful punctures inflicted by some mean spirit, we walked down the dirty, sludgy streets where families and the sick meandered by shops and food stalls, mud-splattered, burnt-out cars, tiny repair workshops, drowsy kiosks, rustic shelters. Feet fettered, the possessed paraded like sleepwalkers, in a disturbing, edgy silence.

Then we headed to the sanctuary where Khadija was respectfully welcomed in the doorway by a local guard, apparently sick as well. The yard was black with people and we mingled with pilgrims and possessed crowded into the entrance to the saint's sepulchre, queueing to touch a heavy chain placed in the sheepskin stretched over the green cloth in the window, and walking round and round a catafalque similarly draped in green. Offerings and ex-votos hung from the walls of the mausoleum. Contrary to what I feared, nobody noticed my presence or fixed me with the evil eye.

As we left, my friend stopped to chat with the sanctuary's keeper and asked after Eusebio. The old man knew no one by this name, only a European, stricken incurably dumb and confined for some time in Buya Omar's prison without bars. He roamed the streets vacant, averse to human warmth, self-preoccupied, unshod, his djellaba frayed, tied to the place by an invisible chain. He wandered, so he said, among the tombs in the cemetery, sought out the dark recesses of caves and shrines, took refuge in the *zawiya* and praying of litanies, a sobbing mass, soaked in sweat. He didn't know who he was, where he was or what he was doing. The echoes of nighttime dirges – the wails, the howls, the laments – fanned the fire of his visions till he fell into a trance. Convulsed by his tortured dreams, he conceived of the world as a huge prison: a string of prisoners, brutal thrashings, human clusters joined by a communitarian chain, a dislocated centipede with extra shackles and ties, that I'd surely read about somewhere?

I felt really perplexed, as if infected by my stay in Buya Omar: during the annual procession to the saint, had Eusebio drunk the miraculous water spurting from the spot

where the saint used to take refuge, a few metres from the
usually dry river; retraced the route signalled by flickering
candles through the labyrinth of criss-crossing smoke-
blackened caves?, followed the rite of the seven turns, from
right to left, anti-clockwise?, appeared before the
sanctuary's Hidden Tribunal opposite which the constable
rubs the heavy chain from the windowsill over the
possessed body, coiling it round his neck with one of
the links hanging from the grille? Had he been submitted
to the interrogation of the spirit possessing him by the judge
invested with the Morabite's esoteric authority so it
revealed its identity, set out its demands, clarified the reasons
behind its aggression against the man beside himself? Did
Eusebio shake like the sick man Khadija saw with her own
eyes, frenzied, shaking because of the undesirable guest's
resistance to the powers of the Hidden Court? Did he have
to be immobilised hands and feet as in our psychiatric
asylums and inquisitional prisons? Did he turn thrice with
his iron collar round the catafalque? Did he remain
enchained while the spirit howled and laughed hysterically,
struggled with the fetters, damning the saint and raining
insults down on him?

According to Khadija, the Hidden Court listens to the
intruder's arguments and the possessed's complaints,
negotiates a pact between them, extends the imprisoning to
the final accord. The sick man can have recourse to his
file in the course of his dreams, receive oneiric advice to
shorten the trial procedures, even know the term for his
mental, physical liberation. The easy-going spirit placates its
anger with the sacrifice of a cockerel or sheep; if the error
imputed to the possessed is more serious, he must offer up
an ox. In cases of evil cast by another, the diagnosis is
arduous, the therapy, tough and protracted. The exorcising

of the spell and expulsion of the intruder sometimes takes months or years.

The old man guided us to the bed of the river, to the area of the saint's retreat, visible from a distance through an arch of two slender palms. Some of the possessed wandered down the dry track, over gravel, pebbles and stones; others crossed in front of us not seeing us, absorbed in the bliss or rawness of a vision or in the parched waste of their apartness.

The character we were all after was stretched out on the ground. If his grimy djellaba and hood over his head were similar to those worn by other sick people, his features were those of a sixty-year-old European: aquiline nose, light-coloured eyes, thin lips slavering at the corners. I crouched down to greet him and got no answer. His gaze passed through me as if my existence were an illusion: an insignificant shadow on the motley face of the universe. The insistent repetition of his name produced no effect. We travelled in different orbits, with no possible meeting point. Immersed in his world, he stared at the chains round his ankles obliquely, almost horizontally.

Was he the same pious man who, according to the old man's patter, regularly came to prayers in the Mosque, had memorised the Koran and was re-reading a much-thumbed copy of the works of Ibn Arabi?

Out of pure desperation, I whispered the words of a Falangist hymn in his ear and he didn't flinch. Nor did the name of Basilio provoke a reaction. When I'd almost given up and was about to get up, deeply moved, I suddenly discovered that his eyes had filled with tears. He cried, silently cried. Then mumbled, almost inaudibly, a single word.

I leave to you, colleagues in the Readers' Circle, the task of guessing it or shall I reveal it?

For a few seconds only, on this occasion, allow me to
keep you in suspense.

It was the title of an old song we've already evoked:
'Rocío', simply 'Rocío'.

# LAAM

All the hypotheses and digressions over Eusebio's stay in the
ancient Almohad capital, irrespective of the greater or lesser
talent with which they were argued, are in my view
gratuitous or circumscribed by severely blinkered vision.

I futilely sniffed after his spoor down winding Medina
side-alleys; in the Square's hustle and bustle, the souks and
poor neighbourhoods; in *zawiyas*, hermitages and even
abandoned cemeteries, a space much favoured, according
to some colleagues, by mysterious witchcraft and spells.

Forgive my forthrightness: such enquiries are trapped, in
my opinion, in a rancid, picturesque banality, in that *couleur
locale* Western travellers are so fond of, particularly the more
neighbourly, borderly members of the species. Given my
ignorance of the Arab world and exclusive interest in our
own matrix, I decided to end my unfruitful meandering
and settle down comfortably in the old French quarter of
Gueliz.

Just one more tourist, I sat under the arcades of the Café
des Négociants, with my good friend Abu Ayub the
chemist or contemplated the splendid panorama of the city
– the Koutoubia, palm grove, snowy peaks of the Atlas
mountains – from the vantage-point or cockpit of the Café
Renaissance. If Eusebio was really in that place, I
concluded, he'd have done exactly the same: seek out

compliant companions in places serving alcohol, though
our tastes and inclinations in things sexual, not wishing to
cause him offence, bent towards different, not to say,
opposite goals.

One morning, guided by confused memories of a dream,
I walked round the Christian cemetery inaugurated when
the first settlers arrived, in the shadow of Lyautey's troops.
Although it was open to the public, I was the only visitor.
For an hour I strolled leisurely between pretentious
gravestones and tombs, till my gaze came to rest on one
eye-catching epitaph: *Alphonse van Worden, 1903–1972*.
After much probing of my grey matter, I realised it
belonged to the protagonist of one of my favourite novels:
*The Saragossa Manuscript*. As you can imagine, my
astonishment spurred me on and my fantasy ran wild over
Potocki's hero and a possible posthumous existence, after
his entry into the pantheon of Don Quixote, Jacques and
his servant, Tristram Shandy and their lesser offspring. The
idea of a hypothetical link to Eusebio only hit my
imagination later. Impelled by another dream – I was
reading Ibn Arabi, at the insistence of my co-readers and
friends! – I returned to the cemetery, went and greeted
the caretaker and, thanks to a story about a relative buried
there twenty years ago and the generous prompt of a handy
tip, the old man allowed me to consult the register of entries
corresponding to 1972. I anxiously inspected the pages:
Alphonse van Worden did not figure there. About to give
up, throw in the towel and say goodbye to the old man, I
was struck by the first name and surname of one of those
interred and its startling coincidence with those of
Eusebio's double as mentioned in a story told by some of my
colleagues: Eugenio Asensio, born in the Canaries,
deceased in Marrakesh, on exactly the same dates inscribed
on the epitaph!

I rushed to the gathering in the Café des Négociants, avoided becoming entangled myself in the nets of the ever-present, ever-ready Madame S., and at a table far from her, by myself, I questioned my friend Abu Ayub. After an initial bucket of cold water – he hadn't met or heard of any Eugenio Asensio – he reassured me by mentioning one of his coffee-drinking colleagues – deservedly celebrated as a snooper and informer – who could dish the dirt on the miraculous doings of Alphonse van Worden, an extraordinarily extravagant exemplar of the city's European fauna.

'Who didn't know, by sight or at the very least by hearsay, Alphonse van Worden, a supposed descendant of Count Potocki, whose glorious title he flaunted, printed on his visiting cards, in a ridiculous display of vainglory?'

(My new interlocutor had all the appearances of a *bon viveur* fond of the pleasures of the vine and the table. Could that be why he gravitated to the orbit of Madame S. and her starred restaurant?)

'He lived in a *riad* in the Bab Dukkala district and would drink himself silly in the bar at the Mamounia, where he repaired daily in his aristocratic, vintage model Rolls, driven by his diminutive, Hindu turbaned chauffeur.

'He made every possible and impossible effort to attract attention and yet wrap himself in an aura of mystery, as if to forge a myth of himself as a noble, at once sober and decadent, initiated in the arcana of Art and Literature.

'He aspired to be a poet, a writer of bold, cryptic lines, their enigma, like Egyptian hieroglyphics, only susceptible to be unravelled by some erudite, tenacious Steiner, versed in the riddles of the esoteric. As these poems never surfaced on his death and the universal heir to his wealth – the pseudo-Hindu chauffeur – declared one day they could only see the light of day ten centuries later, and the day after that his master had ordered they be buried in a cask inlaid with ivory and mother-of-pearl on a bare mountainside in the foothills of the Atlas, I deduce they never existed and that, like his title and ancestors, were strictly his invention.

'He said he was of German-Polish stock, but the fact is he mastered neither language. One afternoon – while he was drinking alone, as usual, in the bar at the Mamounia – I spitefully dispatched an agricultural engineer and native of Danzig to say hello and clear up my doubts, and he confirmed that the would-be van Worden understood not one iota of his greetings and wriggled out of the tight corner in painful, confused French.

'His accent clearly revealed a Maltese or Spanish provenance and, driven by my innate curiosity, I profited from one of my business trips to Casablanca, to collect from diverse sources whatever information I could on a personage of his characteristics: obese, gluttonous, heavy-drinking, exhibitionist, silent, mercurial. Yes, my good friend, he combined all that, a being comprised of elements and features that were not only disparate but even opposed: a chameleon with froggy leanings, plump, bulging eyes, a sickly, wart-ridden skin. Grist to the mill of a latter-day Balzac who could have written a gripping blockbuster *là-dessus*!

'In fact, he was a Spanish trader who'd come from Tangiers. According to unsubstantiated gossip, he'd worked for the secret services of the colonial Vichy administration and hence established the necessary wheeling-and-dealing to get rich quick. He didn't hide his sympathies for Franco and Pétain, but, after the Allies landed, he changed coats and got well in with the Americans. He joined forces with a wily, corruptible officer in Supplies and soon meta-morphosed into a king of the black market. Commissions and merchandise of all kinds regularly passed through his hands and swelled his already respectable coffers. *"Monsieur Eugène"* made and unmade, bought and re-sold, accumulated property and goods as eagerly as he downed pastries in the city's best cake-shops.

'And one day he disappeared, just as he had disappeared from Tangiers. He wound up his business and changed skin. Once in Marrakesh he was Alphonse van Worden, aristocrat, central European and poet. He dressed eccentrically and showed off in his turban-driven Rolls.

'Apart from his religious devotion to the chapel-bar at the Mamounia, he hardly left his *riad*. He'd brought with him a modern film projector and hour after hour wallowed in his favourite films, sprawled on a sofa, holding hands with his Philippine. He loved the musicals starring Raquel Meller and Imperio Argentina, whose names one of his servants scrawled on a piece of paper after I bribed him. He also professed great admiration for Greta Garbo, Joan Crawford and Gloria Swanson: apparently video tapes of them, whether dubbed into French or in the original I know not, occupied place of honour in his film library.

'One night when he'd drunk more than he could handle, he embarked on a version of *The Violet Seller* in the hotel lobby, his reedy tones and grotesque gestures astonishing the clientele, bemusing and stunning the staff – concierge and dickie-bowed porter included – whom he normally showered with notes, in significant contrast to his uncharitable contempt for those wearing the livery of poverty out in the street. He remained in reception like a diva awaiting her ovation, until the Philippine or pseudo-Hindu managed to direct his steps to the renowned, now defunct, canopied entrance, a few metres from his Rolls Royce.

'But the most infamous episode – small talk of the *crème Chantilly* in Gueliz and the spacious villas of the Hivernage

– took place in his own house. Though he kept it veiled from all prying eyes, he invited a select band of more or less aristocratic worthies from the Gotha or Goya of the nobility to a dressy reception to which, most definitely, a Madame S. (sick to the gills), was not invited. Fifteen or twenty penguins or geriatrics, befeathered in tawdry rags and tatters, thus presented themselves at the appointed hour in the alley and were escorted by red-fezzed, white-djellabaed flunkeys to seats arrayed in the stalls opposite the staircase-stage to be immediately attended by waiters with trays of cold drinks, glasses of champagne and canapés of caviar. A reception with nothing spared like in the good old days of Lyautey and Guillaume! Only Count Potocki held back, while the anxious, nimble Philippine saw to the decor, issued sing-song instructions to the servants in respect of the right lighting for the banister and proper placing for the carpet, a personal gift, he whispered, from the Empress of Iran.

'Monsieur Alphonse van Worden, or rather, Madame van Worden, finally appeared – luridly lip-sticked, in blond wig and loose-sleeved organdy suit – to descend the majestic staircase, ready for a gala ball but without her cane, a truly autumnal dame, from Sunset Boulevard or Copacabana, highlighted by hummingbird or bird of Paradise in her solemn, teetering trajectory across the proscenium of immortality. Her erratic zig-zags, verging on total collapse, exposed her true state: the dearie was totally drunk.

'From this moment on, versions diverge. Some say she stumbled, cracked her skull and had to be helped. Others, that she threatened and hurled abuse at her guests: "*Salauds, c'est vous les coupables! A cause des crapules comme vous j'ai gâchée complètement ma vie! Je suis un pantin, une ruine de moi-même, un cadavre puant! Je vous crache et je vous vomis dessus!*"

'When the curtain fell and the scandalised audience

dispersed, the so-called Count Potocki sobbed and sobbed, whimpered uncontrollably, among the deserted stalls.

'The performance was at an end and almost his life too: a few days after the scene I've referred to, a lunatic beggar stabbed Eugenio Asensio to death on the doorstep to his *riad*.'

# MEEM

Yes, I did meet Monsieur Eugène, alias Alphonse van Worden, a Polish aristocrat supposedly of Potocki stock: he was an original, sometimes over-the-top character who, from the day he arrived in Marrakesh in the last years of the Protectorate and purchased a beautiful *riad* – a fine nose for business – from an almost moribund French widow, his ostentatious extravagances won over the European fauna flourishing at the time. His most prominent personality trait consisted of an exquisite blend of arrogance and Mittymania. He posed as prince, poet, artist, as a spy in the pay of the Intelligence Service and a few other roles besides. Daily he constructed himself a character and lived it with the conviction of an actor on stage. His family tree, which he later had etched on leather by an expert artisan from the Medina, went back to the first kings of Poland and related him to the flower of the European aristocracy. Dressed as a count, with his Rolls Royce and ineffable Philippine chauffeur, he'd visit his 'cousin', the Princess of Ruspoli in her mansion in the Urika valley and have his photo taken with her, sitting on the edge of her bed, her entire collection of lapdogs prettily lined up on the quilt. He maintained a real or imaginary correspondence with various uncrowned monarchs, and pretended he owned the copy of *The Duino Elegies*, signed by Rilke, and bequeathed

to him by the noble dedicatee. He'd occasionally take off
on trips to exchange words, or so he said, with his relatives,
the kings of Georgia and Albania. He particularly prided
himself on being a great poet: in his youth, he'd written
verse, confiscated in Spain during the civil war, when he
was arbitrarily interned in a refugee camp, sometimes
he said by Reds and other times by Francoists. According
to what I recently read in the press, these poems turned
up in an out-of-the-way military archive in Melilla and got
into the hands of a rag-and-bone man who sold them for
a song to a Catalan philologist. I don't know whether those
labours had any of life's vital juices. The works he
perpetrated in Marrakesh were worthy candidates for the
shredder if not the gallows. He unashamedly plagiarised
Cavafi and, worse still, interleaved his lines with ones he'd
concocted with words from songs of stars he admired, from
Raquel Meller to Miguel Molina. He'd declaim them
melodramatically, when drunk, to a less than full audience:
his Philippine chauffeur and secretary and yours truly. His
rococo salon suffocated newcomers with a profusion of
furniture, carpets, vases, all manner of refined or kitsch
bric-à-brac. The walls sported photos of the Meller dame,
Imperio Argentina and a galaxy of would-be artists and
genuine crooners whose names escape me. Rather than a
salon, the room and its permanently closed windows
impregnated with aromas of sandalwood or incense, looked
like a diva's luxurious dressing-room, packed with faded
glories and distant memories. On the nights he didn't go to
the bar in the Mamounia and stayed at home, the
Philippine projected his favourite films on the screen, not
only those quoted from hearsay in my colleague's dubious
report, but the showings of many others to which I received
innumerable invitations. Monsieur Eugène watched every
video moment as if it were the first time he'd seen it: he

sighed, belched, threw out compliments and stuffed down pastries. It's true that he and his friend sprawled on the sofa hand-in-hand, but my co-reader's source couldn't see what I could of the succession of disguises they donned according to a film's contents: one soirée, with tux and cane; another, in Egyptian wigs; another, dressed as hussars. Monsieur Eugène collected a wide range of garbs, from cabaret Cinderellas to their excellent majesties, the King and Queen of Bulgaria. Later, once the film was over, they gossiped, commented on dramatic twists and turns, gave full rein to their associations of ideas and erudite memories. They argued over small details in the *artistes'* biographies, their dates of birth, the name of the cameraman and directors of photography. These jousts lasted hours and I acted the guest of stone, but wasn't bored; on the contrary, the tit-bits exchanged by that singular couple allowed me to glimpse a world which, for a discreet homosexual like myself, seemed fascinating and surreal. I was his official companion and wasn't allowed the slightest infidelity. I remember how one night an early morning call woke me up with a start. 'Come now!' Eugène told me, 'We're watching my favourite Mary Pickford video!' It was bitterly cold, I had a streaming nose and wasn't attracted by the idea of abandoning my bed, getting dressed and looking for a taxi to take me to Bab Dukkala. I replied that I was ill and needed to stay in bed. He put the phone down on me and ignored me for several weeks. 'You refused to watch Mary Pickford with me! The one and only Mary Pickford! Not even God could forgive that!' But, more indulgent than the Almighty, he welcomed me back to his intimate world, to the dark, freshly fumigated bosom of his chapel of celluloid, for Eugène suffered from asthma. Like Proust, and just like Proust, he treated me with the same condescension Madame Verdurin showed towards the upstart. If he was bored to tears by a film seen too often, the punctilious Philippine stopped the showing, went though a tiptoe dance routine or fetched something from one of the drawers of the mother-of-pearl encrusted sideboard where his master hoarded secret treasures, his little ditties: pure slush, long-winded and vacuous, dredged from previous styles which had been done to death. Unless, as my unfortunate Arabist colleague said, dates dictate otherwise, I reckon they were still warm from one of those tepid-off-the-presses, dead-on-the-page anthologies of new blood, selected and prologued by the latest laureate or ritual cheer-leader. Their author listened in ecstasy, attentively followed every rhapsodic move and gesture, drunkenly applauding his trills and wiping away his tears. Nevertheless, one tense, sour evening, Eugène or Eugenio interrupted the declamation with a '*non, non, non, tout ça ne vaut rien, c'est de la merde en poudre!*' He slumped on the sofa and had to be helped up to breathe in the salts the Philippine anxiously offered him. '*Eugène, tu te trompes, tu es un génie, un génie incompris qu'on découvrira un jour, comme Lautréamont ou Van Gogh!*' Our man whimpered, looked at himself in a pocket-mirror, readjusted his wig, sought out my agreement. 'Yes, your friend's right, one day your work will be recognised': these words or others of a similar nature sprang inanely from my lips at the spectacle of staged self-pity and infantile guile. For even in his moments of spasmodic, on-the-sleeve sincerity, Eugène lied. It was all part of a display aimed at the gallery, a parade of self-pitying sleaze with which he hid the truth of his life: the years as child, adolescent and youth which preceded the civil war and showed in a harsh light the brutal reality of a stubborn, vicious, cruel, blood-thirsty country. One day, while I was waiting in the salon for the Philippine to dress and spruce him up, I leisurely riffled the drawers of the sideboard, and found the blurred photo of a burly mountain man sporting a crook's exuberant moustache. Without hiding my evil deed and reprehensible curiosity, I asked him who this was. 'An *askari* who helped me and died,' he said, putting the photo back. I couldn't extract another word from him about that fellow. The key, no doubt, to one of the riddles of his life. The fact was all the more shocking in that the sixty-plus, worldly, affected Eugenio, professed a visceral contempt for the natives, who he always called Mustafa. An aversion verging on monomania: he never returned his neighbours' greetings, swore at the poor, ordered the Philippine to speed after pedestrians and laughed at their panicky, startled jumps. In the Mamounia he handed out generous tips and surrounded himself in an odious atmosphere of sycophancy. His lack of pity for the old and needy was by now proverbial in the district: eventually, nobody approached him. That's why I was intrigued a few days before his death by the presence in the rather quiet alley of his *riad* of a beggar who was probably out of his mind, wearing a threadbare djellaba, its hood covering the top part of his face: he lay there still, staring into the distance, almost horizontally, as recently described. I saw him look up for a few seconds as the Philippine opened the garage door and Eugenio – or should I call him Eusebio? – was driving out in his Rolls: a fleeting reflection of eyes flashing hatred, a grudge as keen as the cutting edge of a dagger.

I put the question to you discreetly: was it himself or his double?

# NUUN

My margin for manoeuvre's limited: I drew the short straw, have to conclude our Circle's collective story, bring to a close these lively weeks of garden entertainment; I'll strive to do so from the point where my colleague broke off, if not lineally, at least in a multi-valenced vision of the crime's inevitability.

The varied, confused documentation I collected about our character – in his double version – muddied rather than clarified the incident: press-cuttings from the time, from *Le Matin* – 'Suspicious murder of aristocrat' – and *L'Opinion* – 'One of the real characters of Marrakesh society, famous for his eccentric behaviour, stabbed by a lunatic in the entrance to his mansion' – mention M. Eugène Asensio, a Spanish, ex-pat resident; the Philippine servant's statements on the attack on the Very Noble Sir Alphonse van Worden prove entangled and abstruse without the musical accompaniment of his trills, butterfly flutter and dance steps; an eye-witness version from a post-worker who happened to motorbike by, maintains that the victim ran towards the disturbed element, although the latter was flourishing a knife and clearly intended to attack him. As for the so-called assassin – described as 'without identity papers', 'mad', 'silent', 'totally unrelated to the victim, whom he was probably seeing for the first time' – the extracts from the police report and trial proceedings sentencing him to perpetual confinement in a special centre for the mentally disturbed underline his 'total indifference, apathy, rejection of the world, impassivity, calm acceptance of his sentence'. I was disturbed by the wording of one clerk – 'he seems reasonable but to lack reason': wasn't it perhaps a simple transcription of *budali*, Ibn Arabi's poor in spirit or God's fool?

How can one relate the crossing of the different stations separating visible and invisible realities and reach in one flight the unknown world of transcendence, the double circumstance of a being split by the occurrences of life and fantasies of the narrative even in his own unique spiritual core?

A town-planner's query elicits no answer from the saint. At a stroke I entered the skin of Eusebio: the obese, histrionic, contemptible character we endow him with and his cringing, implacable consciousness. I saw myself with merciless clarity through eyes that were no longer mine: dressed OscarWildly, in straw-boater, bow-tie, a flower in my buttonhole, disguised for one of my dutiful visits to the cheapjack nobility and stars of *Hello* or *Semana*. Half-stretched out on the ground, my head leaning against a wall, I slowly examined the invisible manacles attached to my ankles. Had I just suffered one of the electric shocks prescribed by the resident management and snapped the straps tying me to the bed? Had I sought refuge, like the melancholy wits or those stricken by a theophanous vision, in the village of Tesaut, inhabited only by demented or tormented souls? What dark premonition or narrative device guided me to the alley in Bab Dukkala, where dwelled the incarnation of my wrongs, the personification of my schizophrenia? Fleetingly I relived a series of snapshots of my capture and internment in the hospital barracks in Melilla, of the luminous image of the *askari*, of closeness to

Basilio, periods of harassment and terror, interrogation by
a judge, betrayal of my friend: the different threads of the
story that comprises my life suddenly came together,
reunited what was scattered, harmonised opposites. I didn't
know whether I had been shunted out of my cell with the
help of my faithful companion from the Rif or had gone
along with the stages of descent into such vile, humiliating
abysses. Was it him or was it me? Who looked at who? Was
I brandishing the knife I held so tightly against myself? I
could see it shining in the sun, a redemptive symbol of my
abjection annd condemnation. Obliquely, almost
horizontally, I watched the Philippine as he opened the
garage door, and I, yes, it was I, peered into the street,
clapped eyes on myself, seemed startled by the encounter,
the incendiary brilliance of my eyes, the knife with which
I was preparing to attack, blinded like a moth by the intensity
of the light, running towards it, towards the stabs he was
inflicting, blows, blows, more blows, rapture not pain, there
was no attacked or attacker, the weapon united us both in
joy and exultation, ended the story, full-stopped my life.

Dead men can't talk, so be it.

# HAA

My voice comes from beyond the grave: forced to die by
lots, I trust that a hint of the love and understanding which
modulated it in life filters from the subtle realm to the world
that is still yours. I imagined I was a fictitious character, a
mere paper being like the one you're laboriously
constructing: impotent, fragmented, dispersed, resigned to
the whims of our precarious, unreal condition. I wandered,
absently, through dream scenarios, shaken by sudden
changes and turn-arounds, in a state of stupor and lethargy
similar to that produced by chemicals and the savage therapy
of electric surges. But this time I confronted not nurses, not
psychiatrists, but a monster with repulsive heads: as many
as there were readers in the Circle. I felt watched from a
thousand angles and sides, harassed by a prismatic gaze,
a multiple, polyhedral eye. Impossible to slip off the clasp
cutting into me, to break the web imprisoning me. The only
certainty was reduced to a name which I clung to like a
red-hot nail. If the Andalusian Moll enjoyed the privilege
of being on familiar terms with her author and Unamuno
and Pirandello's characters rebelled audaciously against their
destinies, what could a variegated, fragile entity like myself
do before a gathering of readers creating and destroying
me, propping me up, thumping me. Could the mental
disarray I suffered be cured by the electric shocks and

sedatives being administered? I thought I was back in Melilla, surrounded by a chorus of Fates, bad-mouthing my ideological deviation and nefast behaviour. What most saddened me were the long parentheses of oblivion allocated to other past periods more pleasant to remember. Why that silence around my sister and the beautiful complicity uniting us? I needed to return to relive the years I enjoyed with her: piano lessons, listening to Schubert, Schumann and Brahms. That affinity and conviviality, which were not destroyed by her marriage to a career officer with feelings and ideas entirely opposed to mine, were the real axis of my whole life. Only the evocation of the notes on the piano could save me from so much gloom and misery. But none of the co-readers made that simple gesture of pity towards me. They abandoned me, unaided, to the barren plain of my drought, with no marshes, bulrushes or reeds, didn't even refer to the twenty years of happiness with my saviour and companion in joy and sorrow: Driss, Driss Abu Al Fadail was his name, any reader can check that by visiting his grave next to mine in a steep rural cemetery in the district of Tanahaut. My systematically camouflaged moments of happiness, shade and leafy plenty also included my fruitful friendship with Madame S. Because of the manifest misogyny of some of the Circle's readers, her character has been mercilessly slandered, stripped of its generous qualities and talent. I don't know if she'd exercised the trade of bawd in her youth in the shadow of a braggart from the High Command: the fact is that, when I arrived in the Medina of the Seven Saints, she was a cultured woman who sought out the company of artists and poets, a friend of Denise Masson and musicologist Maurice Fleuret, patron of fledgling painters and publishers of analects in Arabic and French. I, the real Eusebio, declare that the portrait drawn of her contains gross errors and obscene

slanders. Thanks to Madame S. I was able to re-establish
contact with my sister and thus weave the thread of an
intimacy interrupted by war and my brother-in-law's
implacable censorship. Although my present vulnerability
to the pens of the hydra prevents me from disclosing their
contents, our correspondence exists and the letters I
received from her were buried with me in the sepulchre
near Mulay Brahim's mausoleum. The co-readers who
knifed Madame S. didn't stop to mention the person
who became her inseparable friend when she was widowed:
Alice, the pianist and insightful interpreter of the same scores
which cradled my Andalusian childhood and adolescence.
The soothing balm of the soirées in her beautiful *riad* in the
Casbah brings to mind the delicate therapy of the Seleucid
monarchs, when they calmed the sick and demented in their
kingdom with spiritual concerts played by their best
musicians. Doesn't this approach to solace and tranquility
through wind or string instruments, also used by the old
Maristans of Fez and Cairo, perhaps display a better
understanding of human pain and grief than the cruel re-
education to which I was submitted? But I don't want to
conclude my intervention as a readeress on behalf of
Eusebio's bones or ashes without touching a raw nerve: I
met the pasha's cook and can confirm that, just as my
companion and Circle member related, her gastronomic
specialities lived up to the legend. Our slanderous colleague
didn't taste, as I did, her exquisite tagine, vegetable couscous,
or noodles, or her infinite variety of sweets and sweetness:
the day he turned up in Madame S.'s restaurant, already
more than tipsy, she threw him out in the street. Ill-will's
no guide and, after rehearsing refrain and tale, I return
proudly to my grave.

# WAW

Before breaking up, the Readers' Circle invented an author.
After prolonged discussions in which its members showed
off their vast etymological, historical and linguistic
knowledge, they forged a rather fancy Iberian-Basque
surname, Goitisolo, Goitizolo, Goytisolo – the last one
finally won the day – put a Juan in front – Lackland,
Landless, the Baptist, the Apostle? – granted him a place
and date of birth – 1931, year of the Republic, and
Barcelona, a city drawn by lots – , wrote an apocryphal
biography and imputed to him the creation – or
desecration? – of thirty-odd books. When it was time for
goodbyes, when they had tired of the fiction of those weeks
in the garden and longed to return to their family hearths,
in a clever montage, they composed a face from different
images and, to hit the nail on the head, stuck it like a rag
doll, on the flap of the book's jacket.

# YAA

**Books read by the Readers' Circle**
*The Spanish Bawd* by Fernando de Rojas
*Burlesque Songbook*
*The Andalusian Moll* by Francisco Delicado
*Penitence in Love* by Pedro Manuel Ximénez de Urrea
*Don Quixote and Entremeses* by Cervantes
*The Complete Works* of Quevedo
*The Illuminations of Mecca and Contemplations of the Mysteries*
by Ibn Arabi
*The Saragossa Manuscript* by Jean Potocki

**Appropriations and borrowings by co-readers from**
Rafael Basterra
Francisco Bonmatí de Codecido
Ernesto Burgos
Luis Camacho Carrasco
Rafael Duyos
Agustín de Foxá
Ernesto Giménez Caballero
Ramiro Ledesma Ramos
Eduardo Marquina
Eugenio Montes
José María Pemán
José Antonio Primo de Rivera

Luys Santamarina
Víctor de la Serna
Antonio Vallejo Nágera
Fermín Yzurdiaga

in the *Songbook of the War, Ballads of Love and War, Poetic Anthology of the Uprising, Garland of Sonnets in Honour of José Antonio Primo de Rivera*

*idem*, in *Commitment in Spanish Poetry* by J. Lechner and *Spanish Fascist Literature* by Julio Rodríguez Puértolas

'Self-criticism', by Heberto Padilla, *Libre*, 1971
'A letter' from Vicente Aleixandre, *Vuelta*, November 1995

*To Monique, whose presence*
*illumined the male and female readers*
*in the Circle*
*throughout the telling*
*of this Garden of Secrets*